Threads of Grey

Myrtle Reed

Alpha Editions

This edition published in 2023

ISBN : 9789357946971

Design and Setting By
Alpha Editions
www.alphaedis.com
Email - info@alphaedis.com

How the World Watches the
New Year Come In

The proverbial "good resolutions" of the first of January which are usually forgotten the next day, the watch services in the churches, and the tin horns in the city streets, are about the only formalities connected with the American New Year. The Pilgrim fathers took no note of the day, save in this prosaic record: "We went to work betimes"; but one Judge Sewall writes with no small pride of the blast of trumpets which was sounded under his window, on the morning of January 1st, 1697.

He celebrated the opening of the eighteenth century with a very bad poem which he wrote himself, and he hired the bellman to recite the poem loudly through the streets of the town of Boston; but happily for a public, even now too much wearied with minor poets, the custom did not become general.

In Scotland and the North of England the New Year festivities are of great importance. Weeks before hand, the village boys, with great secrecy, meet in out of the way places and rehearse their favourite songs and ballads. As the time draws near, they don improvised masks and go about from door to door, singing and cutting many quaint capers. The thirty-first of December is called "Hogmanay," and the children are told that if they go to the corner, they will see a man with as many eyes as the year has days. The children of the poorer classes go from house to house in the better districts, with a large pocket fastened to their dresses, or a large shawl with a fold in front.

Each one receives an oaten cake, a piece of cheese, or sometimes a sweet cake, and goes home at night heavily laden with a good supply of homely New Year cheer for the rest of the family.

The Scottish elders celebrate the day with a supper party, and as the clock strikes twelve, friend greets friend and wishes him "a gude New Year and mony o' them."

Then with great formality the door is unbarred to let the Old Year out and the New Year in, while all the guests sally forth into the streets to "first foot" their acquaintances.

The "first foot" is the first person to enter a house after midnight of December 31st. If he is a dark man, it is considered an omen of good fortune. Women generally are thought to bring ill luck, and in some parts of England a light-haired man, or a light-haired, flat-footed man is preferred. In Durham, this person must bring a piece of coal, a piece of iron, and a bottle of whiskey. He gives a glass of whiskey to each man and kisses each woman.

In Edinburgh, a great crowd gathers around the church in Hunter Square and anxiously watches the clock. There is absolute silence from the first stroke of twelve until the last, then the elders go to bed, but the young folks have other business on hand. Each girl expects the "first foot" from her sweetheart and there is occasionally much stratagem displayed in outwitting him and arranging to have some grandmother or serving maid open the door for him.

During the last century, all work was laid aside on the afternoon of the thirty-first, and the men of the hamlet went to the woods and brought home a lot of juniper bushes. Each household also procured a pitcher of water from "the dead and living ford," meaning a ford in the river by which passengers and funerals crossed. This was brought in perfect silence and was not allowed to touch the ground in its progress as contact with the earth would have destroyed the charm.

The next morning, there were rites to protect the household against witchcraft, the evil eye, and other machinations of his satanic majesty. The father rose first, and, taking the charmed water and a brush, treated the whole family to a generous sprinkling, which was usually acknowledged with anything but gratitude.

Then all the doors and windows were closed, and the juniper boughs put on the fire. When the smoke reached a suffocating point, the fresh air was admitted. The cattle were fumigated in the same way and the painful solemnities of the morning were over.

The Scots on the first of the year consult the Bible before breakfast. They open it at random and lay a finger on a verse which is supposed to be, in some way, an augury for the coming year. If a lamp or a candle is taken out of the house on that day, some one will die during the year, and on New Year's day a Scotchman will neither lend, borrow nor give anything whatsoever out of his house, for fear his luck may go with it, and for the same reason the floor must not be swept. Even ashes or dirty water must not be thrown out until the next day, and if the fire goes out it is a sign of death.

The ancient Druids distributed among the early Britons branches of the sacred mistletoe, which had been cut with solemn ceremony in the night from the oak trees in a forest that had been dedicated to the gods.

Among the ancient Saxons, the New Year was ushered in with friendly gifts, and all fighting ceased for three days.

In Banffshire the peat fires are covered with ashes and smoothed down. In the morning they are examined closely, and if anything resembling a human footprint is found in the ashes, it is taken as an omen. If the footprint points towards the door, one of the family will die or leave home during the year. If they point inward, a child will be born within the year.

In some parts of rural England, the village maidens go from door to door with a bowl of wassail, made of ale, roasted apples, squares of toast, nutmeg, and sugar. The bowl is elaborately decorated with evergreen and ribbons, and as they go they sing:

"Wassail, wassail to our town,
The cup is white and the ale is brown,
The cup is made of the ashen tree,
And so is the ale of the good barley.

"Little maid, little maid, turn the pin,
Open the door and let us in;
God be there, God be here;
I wish you all a Happy New Year."

In Yorkshire, the young men assemble at midnight on the thirty-first, blacken their faces, disguise themselves in other ways, then pass through the village with pieces of chalk. They write the date of the New Year on gates, doors, shutters, and wagons. It is considered lucky to have one's property so marked and the revellers are never disturbed.

On New Year's Day, Henry VI received gifts of jewels, geese, turkeys, hens, and sweetmeats. "Good Queen Bess" was fairly overwhelmed with tokens of affection from her subjects. One New Year's morning, she was presented with caskets studded with gems, necklaces, bracelets, gowns, mantles, mirrors, fans, and a wonderful pair of black silk stockings, which pleased her so much that she never afterward wore any other kind.

Among the Romans, after the reformation of the calendar, the first day, and even the whole month, was dedicated to the worship of the god Janus. He was represented as having two faces, and looking two ways—into the past and into the future. In January they offered sacrifices to Janus upon two altars, and on the first day of the month they were careful to regulate their speech and conduct, thinking it an augury for the coming year.

New Year's gifts and cards originated in Rome, and there is a record of an amusing lawsuit which grew out of the custom. A poet was commissioned by a Roman pastry-cook to write the mottoes for the New Year day bonbons. He agreed to supply five hundred couplets for six sesterces, and though the poor poet toiled faithfully and the mottoes were used, the money was not forthcoming. He sued the pastry-cook, and got a verdict, but the cook regarded himself as the injured party. Crackers were not then invented, but we still have the mottoes—those queer heart-shaped things which were the delight of our school-days.

The Persians remember the day with gifts of eggs—literally a "lay out!"

In rural Russia, the day begins as a children's holiday. The village boys get up at sunrise and fill their pockets with peas and wheat. They go from house to house and as the doors are never locked, entrance is easy. They throw the peas upon their enemies and sprinkle the wheat softly upon their sleeping friends.

After breakfast, the finest horse in the little town is decorated with evergreens and berries and led to the house of the greatest nobleman, followed by the pea and wheat shooters of the early morning. The lord admits both horse and people to his house, where the whole family is gathered, and the children of his household make presents of small pieces of silver money to those who come with the horse. This is the greeting of the peasants to their lord and master.

Next comes a procession of domestic animals, an ox, cow, goat, and pig, all decorated with evergreens and berries. These do not enter the house but pass slowly up and down outside, that the master and his family may see. Then the old women of the village bring barnyard fowls to the master as presents, and these are left in the house which the horse has only recently vacated. Even the chickens are decorated with strings of berries around their necks and bits of evergreen fastened to their tails.

The Russians have also a ceremony which is more agreeable. On each New Year's Day, a pile of sheaves is heaped up over a large pile of grain, and the father, after seating himself behind it, asks the children if they can see him. They say they cannot, and he replies that he hopes the crops for the coming year will be so fine that he will be hidden in the fields.

In the cities there is a grand celebration of mass in the morning and the rest of the day is devoted to congratulatory visits. Good wishes which cannot be expressed in person are put into the newspapers in the form of advertisements, and in military and official circles ceremonial visits are paid.

The Russians are very fond of fortune-telling, and on New Year's eve the young ladies send their servants into the street to ask the names of the first person they meet, and many a bashful lover has hastened his suit by taking good care to be the first one who is met by the servant of his lady love. At midnight, each member of the family salutes every other member with a kiss, beginning with the head of the house, and then they retire, after gravely wishing each other a Happy New Year.

Except that picturesque rake, Leopold of Belgium, every monarch of Europe has for many years begun the New Year with a solemn appeal to the Almighty, for strength, guidance, and blessing.

The children in Belgium spend the day in trying to secure a "sugar uncle" or a "sugar aunt." The day before New Year, they gather up all the keys of the household and divide them. The unhappy mortal who is caught napping finds himself in a locked room, from which he is not released until a ransom is offered. This is usually money for sweets and is divided among the captors.

In France, no one pays much attention to Christmas, but New Year's day is a great festival and presents are freely exchanged. The President of France also holds a reception somewhat similar to, and possibly copied from, that which takes place in the White House.

In Germany, complimentary visits are exchanged between the merest acquaintances, and New Year's gifts are made to the servants. The night of the thirty-first is called *Sylvester Aben* and while many of the young people dance, the day in more serious households takes on a religious aspect. During the evening, there is prayer at the family altar, and at midnight the watchman on the church tower blows his horn to announce the birth of the New Year.

At Frankfort-on-the-Main a very pretty custom is observed. On New Year's eve the whole city keeps a festival with songs, feasting, games, and family parties in every house. When the great bell in the cathedral tolls the first stroke of midnight, every house opens wide its windows. People lean from the casements, glass in hand, and from a hundred thousand throats comes the cry: *"Prosit Neujahr!"* At the last stroke, the windows are closed and a midnight hush descends upon the city.

The hospitable Norwegians and Swedes spread their tables heavily; for all who may come in at Stockholm there is a grand banquet at the Exchange, where the king meets his people in truly democratic fashion.

The Danes greet the New Year with a tremendous volley of cannon, and at midnight old Copenhagen is shaken to its very foundations. It is considered a delicate compliment to fire guns and pistols under the bedroom windows of one's friends at dawn of the new morning.

The dwellers in Cape Town, South Africa, are an exception to the general custom of English colonists, and after the manner of the early Dutch settlers they celebrate the New Year during the entire week. Every house is full of visitors, every man, woman, and child is dressed in gay garments, and no one has any business except pleasure. There are picnics to Table Mountain, and pleasure excursions in boats, with a dance every evening. At the end of the week, everybody settles down and the usual routine of life is resumed.

In the Indian Empire, the day which corresponds to our New Year is called "Hooly" and is a feast in honour of the god Krishna. Caste temporarily loses ground and the prevailing colour is red. Every one who can afford it wears red garments, red powder is thrown as if it were *confetti*, and streams of red water are thrown upon the passers-by. It is all taken in good part, however, as snowballing is with us.

Even "farthest North," where the nights are six months long, there is recognition of the New Year. The Esquimaux come out of their snow huts and ice caves in pairs, one of each pair being dressed in women's clothes. They gain entrance into every *igloo* in the village, moving silently and mysteriously. At last there is not a light left in the place, and having extinguished every fire they can find, they kindle a fresh one, going through in the meantime solemn ceremonies. From this one source, all the fires and lights in the district are kindled anew.

One wonders if there may not be some fear in the breasts of these Children of the North, when for an instant they stand in the vastness of the midnight, utterly without fire or light.

The most wonderful ceremonies connected with the New Year take place in China and Japan. In these countries and in Corea the birth of the year is considered the birthday of the whole community. When a child is born he is supposed to be a year old, and he remains thus until the changing seasons bring the annual birthday of the whole Mongolian race, when another year is credited to his account.

In the Chinese quarter of the large cities, the New Year celebrations are dreaded by the police, since where there is so much revelry there is sure to be trouble. In the native country, the rejoicings absorb fully a month, during the first part of which no hunger is allowed to exist within the Empire.

The refreshments are light in kind—peanuts, watermelon seeds, sweetmeats, oranges, tea and cakes. Presents of food are given to the poor, and "brilliant cakes," supposed to help the children in their studies, are distributed from the temples.

The poor little Chinamen must sadly need some assistance, in view of the fact that every word in their language has a distinct root, and their alphabet contains over twenty thousand letters.

At an early hour on New Year's morning, which according to their calendar comes between the twenty-first of January and the nineteenth of February, they propitiate heaven and earth with offerings of rice, vegetables, tea, wine, oranges, and imitation of paper money which they burn with incense, joss-sticks, and candles.

Strips of scarlet paper, bearing mottoes, which look like Chinese laundry checks, are pasted around and over doors and windows. Blue strips among the red, mean that a death has occurred in the family since the last celebration.

New Year's calls are much in vogue in China, where every denizen of the Empire pays a visit to each of his superiors, and receives them from all of his inferiors. Sometimes cards are sent, and, as with us, this takes the place of a call.

Images of gods are carried in procession to the beating of a deafening gong, and mandarins go by hundreds to the Emperor and the Dowager Empress, with congratulatory addresses. Their robes are gorgeously embroidered and are sometimes heavy with gold. After this, they worship their household gods.

Illuminations and fireworks make the streets gorgeous at night, and a monstrous Chinese dragon, spouting flame, is drawn through the streets.

People salute each other with cries of "Kung-hi! Kung-hi!" meaning I humbly wish you joy, or "Sin-hi! Sin-hi!" May joy be yours.

Many amusements in the way of theatricals and illumination are provided for the public.

In both China and Japan, all debts must be paid and all grudges settled before the opening of the New Year. Every one is supposed to have new clothes for the occasion, and those who cannot obtain them remain hidden in their houses.

In Japan, the conventional New Year costume is light blue cotton, and every one starts out to make calls. Letters on rice paper are sent to those in distant places, conveying appropriate greetings.

The Japanese also go to their favourite tea gardens where bands play, and wax figures are sold. Presents of cooked rice and roasted peas, oranges, and figs are offered to every one. The peas are scattered about the houses to frighten away the evil spirits, and on the fourth day of the New Year, the decorations of lobster, signifying reproduction, cabbages indicating riches, and oranges, meaning good luck, are taken down and replaced with boughs of fruit trees and flowers.

Strange indeed is the country in which the milestones of Time pass unheeded. In spite of all the mirth and feasting, there is an undercurrent of sadness which has been most fitly expressed by Charles Lamb:

"Of all the sounds, the most solemn and touching is the peal which rings out the old year. I never hear it without gathering up in my mind a concentration of all the images that have been diffused over the past twelve months; all that I have done or suffered, performed, or neglected, in that regretted time. I begin to know its worth as when a person dies. It takes a personal colour, nor was it a poetical flight in a contemporary, when he exclaimed: 'I saw the skirts of the departing year!'"

The Two Years

Tread softly, ye throngs with hurrying feet,
Look down, O ye stars, in your flight,
And bid ye farewell to a time that was sweet,
For the year lies a-dying to-night.

In a shroud of pure snow lie the quickly-fled hours—
The children of Time and of Light;
Stoop down, ye fair moon, and scatter sweet flowers,
For the year lies a-dying to-night.

Hush, O ye rivers that sweep to the sea,
From hill and from blue mountain height;
The flood of your song should be sorrow, not glee,
For the year lies a-dying to-night.

Good night, and good-bye, dear, mellow, old year,
The new is beginning to dawn.
But we'll turn and drop on thy white grave a tear,
For the sake of the friend that is gone.

All hail to the New! He is coming with gladness,
From the East, where in light he reposes;
He is bringing a year free from pain and from sadness,
He is bringing a June with her roses.

A burst of sweet music, the listeners hear,
The stars and the angels give warning—
He is coming in beauty, this joyful New Year,
O'er the flower-strewn stairs of the morning.

He is bringing a day with glad pulses beating,
For the sorrow and passion are gone,
And Love and Life have a rapturous meeting
In the rush and the gladness of dawn.

The Old has gone out with a crown that is hoary,
The New in his brightness draws near;
Then let us look up in the light and the glory,
And welcome this royal New Year.

The Courtship of George Washington

The quaint old steel engraving which shows George and Martha Washington sitting by a table, while the Custis children stand dutifully by, is a familiar picture in many households, yet few of us remember that the first Lady of the White House was not always first in the heart of her husband.

The years have brought us, as a people, a growing reverence for him who was in truth the "Father of His Country." Time has invested him with godlike attributes, yet, none the less, he was a man among men, and the hot blood of youth ran tumultuously in his veins.

At the age of fifteen, like many another schoolboy, Washington fell in love. The man who was destined to be the Commander of the Revolutionary Army, wandered through the shady groves of Mount Vernon composing verses which, from a critical standpoint, were very bad. Scraps of verse were later mingled with notes of surveys, and interspersed with the accounts which that methodical statesman kept from his school-days until the year of his death.

In the archives of the Capitol on a yellowed page, in Washington's own handwriting, these lines are still to be read:

"Oh, Ye Gods, why should my Poor Resistless Heart
Stand to oppose thy might and Power,
At last surrender to Cupid's feather'd Dart,
And now lays bleeding every Hour
For her that's Pityless of my grief and Woes,
And will not on me, pity take.
I'll sleep amongst my most inveterate Foes,
And with gladness never wish to wake.
In deluding sleepings let my Eyelids close,
That in an enraptured Dream I may
In a soft lulling sleep and gentle repose
Possess those joys denied by Day."

Among these boyish fragments there is also an incomplete acrostic, evidently intended for Miss Frances Alexander, which reads as follows:

"From your bright sparkling Eyes I was undone;
Rays, you have, rays more transparent than the Sun
Amidst its glory in the rising Day;
None can you equal in your bright array;
Constant in your calm, unspotted Mind;
Equal to all, but will to none Prove kind,

So knowing, seldom one so young you'll Find.

"Ah, woe's me that I should Love and conceal—
Long have I wished, but never dare reveal,
Even though severely Love's Pains I feel;
Xerxes that great wast not free from Cupid's Dart,
And all the greatest Heroes felt the smart."

He wrote at length to several of his friends concerning his youthful passions. In the tell-tale pages of the diary, for 1748, there is this draft of a letter:

"DEAR FRIEND ROBIN: My place of Residence is at present at His Lordship's where I might, was my heart disengag'd, pass my time very pleasantly, as there's a very agreeable Young Lady Lives in the same house (Col. George Fairfax's Wife's Sister); but as that's only adding fuel to fire, it makes me the more uneasy, for by often and unavoidably being, in Company with her revives my former Passion for your Lowland Beauty; whereas was I to live more retired from young Women I might in some measure aliviate my sorrows by burying that chaste and troublesome Passion in the grave of oblivion or eternal forgetfulness, for as I am very well assured, that's the only antidote or remedy, that I shall be relieved by, as I am well convinced, was I ever to ask any question, I should only get a denial which would be adding grief to uneasiness."

The "Lowland Beauty" was Miss Mary Bland. Tradition does not say whether or not she ever knew of Washington's admiration, but she married Henry Lee.

"Light Horse Harry," that daring master of cavalry of Revolutionary fame, was the son of the "Lowland Beauty," and some tender memories of the mother may have been mingled with Washington's fondness for the young soldier. It was "Light Horse Harry" also, who said of the Commander-in-Chief that he was "first in war, first in peace, and first in the hearts of his countrymen!"

By another trick of fate the grandson of the "Lowland Beauty" was Gen. Robert E. Lee. Who can say what momentous changes might have been wrought in history had Washington married his first love?

Miss Gary, the sister of Mrs. Fairfax, was the "agreeable young lady" of whom he speaks. After a time her charm seems to have partially mitigated the pain he felt over the loss of her predecessor in his affections. Later he writes of a Miss Betsey Fauntleroy, saying that he is soon to see her, and that he "hopes for a revocation of her former cruel sentence."

When Braddock's defeat brought the soldier again to Mount Vernon, to rest from the fatigues of the campaign, there is abundant evidence to prove that he had become a personage in the eyes of women. For instance, Lord Fairfax writes to him, saying:

"If a Satterday Night's Rest cannot be sufficient to enable your coming hither to-morrow the Lady's will try to get Horses to equip our Chair or attempt their strength on Foot to Salute you, so desirious are they with loving Speed to have an occular Demonstration of your being the same identical Gent— that lately departed to defend his Country's Cause."

A very feminine postscript was attached to this which read as follows:

"DEAR SIR

"After thanking Heaven for your safe return, I must accuse you of great unkindness in refusing us the pleasure of seeing you this night. I do assure you nothing but our being satisfied that our company would be disagreeable, should prevent us from trying if our Legs would not carry us to Mount Vernon this night, but if you will not come to us, to-morrow morning very early we shall be at Mount Vernon.

"SALLY FAIRFAX
ANN SPEARING
ELIZ'TH DENT"

Yet, in spite of the attractions of Virginia we find him journeying to Boston, on military business, by way of New York.

The hero of Braddock's stricken field found every door open before him. He was fêted in Philadelphia, and the aristocrats of Manhattan gave dinners in honour of the strapping young soldier from the wilds of Virginia.

At the house of his friend, Beverly Robinson, he met Miss Mary Philipse, and speedily surrendered. She was a beautiful, cultured woman, twenty-five years old, who had travelled widely and had seen much of the world. He promptly proposed to her, and was refused, but with exquisite grace and tact.

Graver affairs however soon claimed his attention, and he did not go back, though a friend wrote to him that Lieutenant-Colonel Morris was besieging the citadel. She married Morris, and their house in Morristown became Washington's headquarters, in 1776—again, how history might have been changed had Mary Philipse married her Virginia lover!

In the spring of 1758, Washington met his fate. He was riding on horseback from Mount Vernon to Williamsburg with important despatches. In crossing a ford of the Pamunkey he fell in with a Mr. Chamberlayne, who lived in the neighbourhood. With true Virginian hospitality he prevailed upon Washington to take dinner at his house, making the arrangement with much difficulty, however, since the soldier was impatient to get to Williamsburg.

Once inside the colonial house, whose hospitable halls breathed welcome, his impatience, and the errand itself, were almost forgotten. A negro servant led his horse up and down the gravelled walk in front of the house; the servant grew tired, the horse pawed and sniffed with impatience, but Washington lingered.

A petite hazel-eyed woman—she who was once Patsy Dandridge, but then the widow of Daniel Parke Custis—was delaying important affairs. At night-fall the distracted warrior remembered his mission, and made a hasty adieu. Mr. Chamberlayne, meeting him at the door, laid a restraining hand upon his arm. "No guest ever leaves my house after sunset," he said.

The horse was put up, the servant released from duty, and Washington remained until the next morning, when, with new happiness in his heart, he dashed on to Williamsburg.

We may well fancy that her image was before him all the way. She had worn a gown of white dimity, with a cluster of Mayblossoms at her belt, and a little white widow's cap half covered her soft brown hair.

She was twenty-six, some three months younger than Washington; she had wealth, and two children. Mr. Custis had been older than his Patsy, for she was married when she was but seventeen. He had been a faithful and affectionate husband, but he had not appealed to her imagination, and it was doubtless through her imagination, that the big Virginia Colonel won her heart.

She left Mr. Chamberlayne's and went to her home—the "White House"—near William's Ferry. The story is that when Washington came from Williamsburg, he was met at the ferry by one of Mrs. Custis's slaves. "Is your mistress at home?" he inquired of the negro who was rowing him across the river.

"Yes, sah," replied the darkey, then added slyly, "I recon you am de man what am expected."

It was late in the afternoon of the next day when Washington took his departure, but he had her promise and was happy. A ring was ordered from Philadelphia, and is duly set down in his accounts: "One engagement ring, two pounds, sixteen shillings."

Then came weary months of service in the field, and they saw each other only four times before they were married. There were doubtless frequent letters, but only one of them remains. It is the letter of a soldier:

"We have begun our march for the Ohio, [he wrote]. A courier is starting for Williamsburg, and I embrace the opportunity to send a few words to one whose life is now inseparable from mine.

"Since that happy hour, when we made our pledges to each other, my thoughts have been continually going to you as to another self. That an All-powerful Providence may keep us both in safety is the prayer of your ever faithful and affectionate Friend,

"G. WASHINGTON

"20th of July
Mrs. Martha Custis."

On the sixth of the following January they were married in the little church of St. Peter. Once again Dr. Mossum, in full canonicals, married "Patsy" Dandridge to the man of her choice. The bridegroom wore a blue cloth coat lined with red silk and ornamented with silver trimmings. His vest was embroidered white satin, his shoe- and knee-buckles were of solid gold, his hair was powdered, and a dress sword hung at his side.

The bride was attired in heavy brocaded white silk inwoven with a silver thread. She wore a white satin quilted petticoat with heavy corded white silk over-skirt, and high-heeled shoes of white satin with buckles of brilliants. She had ruffles of rich point lace, pearl necklace, ear-rings, and bracelets, and was attended by three bridesmaids.

The aristocracy of Virginia was out in full force. One of the most imposing figures was Bishop, the negro servant, who had led Washington's horse up and down the gravelled path in front of Mr. Chamberlayne's door while the master lingered within. He was in the scarlet uniform of King George's army, booted and spurred, and he held the bridle rein of the chestnut charger that was forced to wait while his rider made love.

On leaving the church, the bride and her maids rode back to the "White House" in a coach drawn by six horses, and guided by black post-boys in livery, while Colonel Washington, on his magnificent horse, and attended by a brilliant company, rode by her side.

There was no seer to predict that some time the little lady in white satin, brocade silk, and rich laces, would spend long hours knitting stockings for her husband's army, and that night after night would find her, in a long grey cloak, at the side of the wounded, hearing from stiffening lips the husky whisper, "God bless you, Lady Washington!"

All through the troublous times that followed, Washington was the lover as well as the husband. He took a father's place with the little children, treating them with affection, but never swerving from the path of justice. With the fondness of a lover, he ordered fine clothes for his wife from London.

After his death, Mrs. Washington destroyed all of his letters. There is only one of them to be found which was written after their marriage. It is in an old book, printed in New York in 1796, when the narrow streets around the tall spire of Trinity were the centre of social life, and the busy hum of Wall Street was not to be heard for fifty years!

One may fancy a stately Knickerbocker stopping at a little bookstall where the dizzy heights of the Empire Building now rise, or down near the Battery, untroubled by the white cliff called "The Bowling Green," and asking pompously enough, for the *Epistles; Domestic, Confidential, and Official, from General Washington.*

The pages are yellowed with age, and the "f" used in the place of the "s", as well as the queer orthography and capitalisation, look strange to twentieth-century eyes, but on page 56 the lover-husband pleads with his lady in a way that we can well understand.

The letter is dated "June 24, 1776," and in part is as follows:

"MY DEAREST LIFE AND LOVE:—

"You have hurt me, I know not how much, by the insinuation in your last, that my letters to you have been less frequent because I have felt less concern for you.

"The suspicion is most unjust; may I not add, is most unkind. Have we lived, now almost a score of years, in the closest and dearest conjugal intimacy to so little purpose, that on the appearance only, of inattention to you, and which you might have accounted for in a thousand ways more natural and more probable, you should pitch upon that single motive which is alone injurious to me?

"I have not, I own, wrote so often to you as I wished and as I ought.

"But think of my situation, and then ask your heart if I be *without excuse?*

"We are not, my dearest, in circumstances the most favorable to our happiness; but let us not, I beseech of you, make them worse by indulging suspicions and apprehensions which minds in distress are apt to give way to.

"I never was, as you have often told me, even in my better and more disengaged days, so attentive to the little punctillios of friendship, as it may be, became me; but my heart tells me, there never was a moment in my life, since I first knew you, in which it did not cleave and cling to you with the warmest affection; and it must cease to beat ere it can cease to wish for your happiness, above anything on earth.

"Your faithful and tender husband, G. W."

"'Seventy-six!" The words bring a thrill even now, yet, in the midst of those stirring times, not a fortnight before the Declaration was signed, and after twenty years of marriage, he could write her like this. Even his reproaches are gentle, and filled with great tenderness.

And so it went on, through the Revolution and through the stormy days in which the Republic was born. There were long and inevitable separations, yet a part of the time she was with him, doing her duty as a soldier's wife, and sternly refusing to wear garments which were not woven in American looms.

During the many years they lived at Mount Vernon, they attended divine service at Christ Church, Alexandria, Virginia, one of the quaint little landmarks of the town which is still standing. For a number of years he was a vestryman of the church, and the pew occupied by him is visited yearly by thousands of tourists while sight-seeing in the national Capitol. Indeed all the churches, so far as known, in which he once worshipped, have preserved his pew intact, while there are hundreds of tablets, statues, and monuments throughout the country.

In the magnificent monument at Washington, rising to a height of more than 555 feet, the various States of the Union have placed stone replicas of their State seals, and these, with other symbolic devices, constitute the inscriptions upon one hundred and seventy-nine of these memorial stones. Not only this, but Europe and Asia, China and Japan have honoured themselves by erecting memorials to the great American.

When at last his long years of service for his country were ended, he and his beloved wife returned again to their beautiful home at Mount Vernon, to wait for the night together. The whole world knows how the end came, with her loving ministrations to the very last of the three restful years which they at this time spent together at the old home, and how he looked Death bravely in the face, as became a soldier and a Christian.

The Old and the New

Grandmother sat at her spinning wheel
In the dust of the long ago,
And listened, with scarlet dyeing her cheeks,
For the step she had learned to know.
A courtly lover, was he who came,
With frill and ruffle and curl—
They dressed so queerly in the days
When grandmother was a girl!

"Knickerbockers" they called them then,
When they spoke of the things at all—
Grandfather wore them, buckled and trim,
When he sallied forth to call.
Grandmother's eyes were youthful then—
His "guiding stars," he said;
While she demurely watched her wheel
And spun with a shining thread.

Frill, and ruffle, and curl are gone,
But the "knickers" are with us still—
And so is love and the spinning wheel,
But we ride it now—if you will!
In grandfather's "knickers" I sit and watch
For the gleam of a lamp afar;
And my heart still turns, as theirs, methinks,
To my wheel and my guiding star.

The Love Story of the "Sage of Monticello"

American history holds no more beautiful love-story than that of Thomas Jefferson, third President of the United States, and author of the Declaration of Independence. It is a tale of single-hearted, unswerving devotion, worthy of this illustrious statesman. His love for his wife was not the first outpouring of his nature, but it was the strongest and best—the love, not of the boy, but of the man.

Jefferson was not particularly handsome as a young man, for he was red-haired, awkward, and knew not what to do with his hands, though he played the violin passably well. But his friend, Patrick Henry, suave, tactful and popular, exerted himself to improve Jefferson's manners and fit him for general society, attaining at last very pleasing results, although there was a certain roughness in his nature, shown in his correspondence, which no amount of polishing seemed able to overcome.

John Page was Jefferson's closest friend, and to him he wrote very fully concerning the state of his mind and heart, and with a certain quaint, uncouth humour, which to this day is irresistible.

For instance, at Fairfield, Christmas day, 1762, he wrote to his friend as follows:

DEAR PAGE

"This very day, to others the day of greatest mirth and jolity, sees me overwhelmed with more and greater misfortunes than have befallen a descendant of Adam for these thousand years past, I am sure; and perhaps, after excepting Job, since the creation of the world.

"You must know, Dear Page, that I am now in a house surrounded by enemies, who take counsel together against my soul; and when I lay me down to rest, they say among themselves, 'Come let us destroy him.'

"I am sure if there is such a thing as a Devil in this world, he must have been here last night, and have had some hand in what happened to me. Do you think the cursed rats (at his instigation I suppose) did not eat up my pocket book, which was in my pocket, within an inch of my head? And not contented with plenty for the present, they carried away my gemmy worked silk garters, and half a dozen new minuets I had just got, to serve, I suppose, as provision for the winter.

"You know it rained last night, or if you do not know it, I am sure I do. When I went to bed I laid my watch in the usual place, and going to take her up after I arose this morning, I found her in the same place, it is true, but all afloat in water, let in at a leak in the roof of the house, and as silent, and as still as the rats that had eaten my pocket book.

"Now, you know if chance had anything to do in this matter, there were a thousand other spots where it might have chanced to leak as well as this one which was perpendicularly over my watch. But I'll tell you, it's my opinion that the Devil came and bored the hole over it on purpose.

"Well, as I was saying, my poor watch had lost her speech. I would not have cared much for this, but something worse attended it—the subtle particles of water with which the case was filled had, by their penetration, so overcome the cohesion of the particles of the paper, of which my dear picture, and watch patch paper, were composed, that in attempting to take them out to dry them, my cursed fingers gave them such a rent as I fear I shall never get over.

"... And now, though her picture be defaced, there is so lively an image of her imprinted in my mind, that I shall think of her too often, I fear for my peace of mind; and too often I am sure to get through old Coke this winter, for I have not seen him since I packed him up in my trunk in Williamsburg. Well, Page, I do wish the Devil had old Coke for I am sure I never was so tired of the dull old scoundrel in my life....

"I would fain ask the favor of Miss Bettey Burwell to give me another watch paper of her own cutting, which I should esteem much more though it were a plain round one, than the nicest in the world cut by other hands; however I am afraid she would think this presumption, after my suffering the other to get spoiled. If you think you can excuse me to her for this, I should be glad if you would ask her...."

Page was a little older than Jefferson, and the young man thought much of his advice. Six months later we find Page advising him to go to Miss Rebecca Burwell and "lay siege in form."

There were many objections to this—first, the necessity of keeping the matter secret, and of "treating with a ward before obtaining the consent of her guardian," which at that time was considered dishonourable, and second, Jefferson's own state of suspense and uneasiness, since the lady had given him no grounds for hope.

"If I am to succeed [he wrote], the sooner I know it the less uneasiness I shall have to go through. If I am to meet with disappointment, the sooner I know it, the more of life I shall have to wear it off; and if I do meet with one, I hope and verily believe it will be the last.

"I assure you that I almost envy you your present freedom and I assure you that if Belinda will not accept of my heart, it shall never be offered to another."

In his letters he habitually spoke of Miss Burwell as "Belinda," presumably on account of the fear which he expresses to Page, that the letters might possibly fall into other hands. In some of his letters he spells "Belinda" backward, and with exaggerated caution, in Greek letters.

Finally, with much fear and trembling, he took his friend's advice, and laid siege to the fair Rebecca in due form. The day afterward—October 7, 1763—he confided in Page:

"In the most melancholy fit that ever a poor soul was, I sit down to write you. Last night, as merry as agreeable company and dancing with Belinda could make me, I never could have thought that the succeeding sun would have seen me so wretched as I now am!

"I was prepared to say a great deal. I had dressed up in my own mind, such thoughts as occurred to me, in as moving language as I knew how, and expected to have performed in a tolerably creditable manner. But ... when I had an opportunity of venting them, a few broken sentences, uttered in great disorder, and interrupted by pauses of uncommon length were the too visible marks of my strange confusion!

"The whole confab I will tell you, word for word if I can when I see you which God send, may be soon."

After this, he dates his letters at "Devilsburg," instead of Williamsburg, and says in one of them, "I believe I never told you that we had another occasion." This time he behaved more creditably, told "Belinda" that it was necessary for him to go to England, explained the inevitable delays and told how he should conduct himself until his return. He says that he asked no questions which would admit of a categorical answer—there was something of the lawyer in this wooing! He assured Miss Rebecca that such a question would one day be asked. In this letter she is called "Adinleb" and spoken of as "he."

Miss Burwell did not wait, however, until Jefferson was in a position to seek her hand openly, but was suddenly married to another. The news was a great shock to Jefferson, who refused to believe it until Page confirmed it; but the love-lorn swain gradually recovered from his disappointment.

With youthful ardour they had planned to buy adjoining estates and have a carriage in common, when each married the lady of his love, that they might attend all the dances. A little later, when Page was also crossed in love, both forswore marriage forever.

For five or six years, Jefferson was faithful to his vow—rather an unusual record. He met his fate at last in the person of a charming widow—Martha Skelton.

The death of his sister, his devotion to his books, and his disappointment made him a sadder and a wiser man. His home at Shadwell had been burned, and he removed to Monticello, a house built on the same estate on a spur of the Blue Ridge Mountains, five hundred feet above the common level.

He went often to visit Mrs. Skelton who made her home with her father after her bereavement. Usually he took his violin under his arm, and out of the harmonies which came from the instrument and the lady's spinet came the greater one of love.

They were married in January of 1772. The ceremony took place at "The Forest" in Charles City County. The chronicles describe the bride as a beautiful woman, a little above medium height, finely formed, and with graceful carriage. She was well educated, read a great deal, and played the spinet unusually well.

The wedding journey was a strange one. It was a hundred miles from "The Forest" to Monticello, and years afterward their eldest daughter, Martha Jefferson Randolph, described it as follows:

"They left 'The Forest' after a fall of snow, light then, but increasing in depth as they advanced up the country. They were finally obliged to quit the carriage and proceed on horseback. They arrived late at night, the fires were all out, and the servants had retired to their own houses for the night. The horrible dreariness of such a house, at the end of such a journey, I have often heard both relate."

Yet, the walls of Monticello, that afterwards looked down upon so much sorrow and so much joy, must have long remembered the home-coming of master and mistress, for the young husband found a bottle of old wine "on a shelf behind some books," built a fire in the open fireplace, and "they laughed and sang together like two children."

And that life upon the hills proved very nearly ideal. They walked and planned and rode together, and kept house and garden books in the most minute fashion.

Births and deaths followed each other at Monticello, but there was nothing else to mar the peace of that happy home. Between husband and wife there was no strife or discord, not a jar nor a rift in that unity of life and purpose which welds two souls into one.

Childish voices came and went, but two daughters grew to womanhood, and in the evening, the day's duties done, violin and harpsichord sounded sweet strains together.

They reared other children besides their own, taking the helpless brood of Jefferson's sister into their hearts and home when Dabney Carr died. Those three sons and three daughters were educated with his own children, and lived to bless him as a second father.

One letter is extant which was written to one of the nieces whom Jefferson so cheerfully supported. It reads as follows:

"PARIS, June 14, 1787.

"I send you, my dear Patsey, the fifteen livres you desired. You propose this to me as an anticipation of five weeks' allowance, but do you not see, my dear, how imprudent it is to lay out in one moment what should accommodate you for five weeks? This is a departure from that rule which I wish to see you governed by, thro' your whole life, of never buying anything which you have not the money in your pocket to pay for.

"Be sure that it gives much more pain to the mind to be in debt than to do without any article whatever which we may seem to want.

"The purchase you have made is one I am always ready to make for you because it is my wish to see you dressed always cleanly and a little more than decently; but apply to me first for the money before making the purchase, if only to avoid breaking through your rule.

"Learn yourself the habit of adhering vigorously to the rules you lay down for yourself. I will come for you about eleven o'clock on Saturday. Hurry the making of your gown, and also your redingcote. You will go with me some day next week to dine at the Marquis Fayette. Adieu, my dear daughter,

"Yours affectionately,
"TH. JEFFERSON"

Mrs. Jefferson's concern for her husband, the loss of her children, and the weary round of domestic duties at last told upon her strong constitution.

After the birth of her sixth child, Lucy Elizabeth, she sank rapidly, until at last it was plain to every one, except the distracted husband, that she could never recover.

Finally the blow fell. His daughter Martha wrote of it as follows:

"As a nurse no female ever had more tenderness or anxiety. He nursed my poor mother in turn with Aunt Carr, and her own sister—sitting up with her and administering her medicines and drink to the last.

"When at last he left his room, three weeks after my mother's death, he rode out, and from that time, he was incessantly on horseback, rambling about the mountain."

Shortly afterward he received the appointment of Plenipotentiary to Europe, to be associated with Franklin and Adams in negotiating peace. He had twice refused the same appointment, as he had promised his wife that he would never again enter public life, as long as she lived.

Columbia

She comes along old Ocean's trackless way—
A warrior scenting conflict from afar
And fearing not defeat nor battle-scar
Nor all the might of wind and dashing spray;
Her foaming path to triumph none may stay
For in the East, there shines her morning star;
She feels her strength in every shining spar
As one who grasps his sword and waits for day.

Columbia, Defender! dost thou hear?
The clarion challenge sweeps the sea
And straight toward the lightship doth she steer,
Her steadfast pulses sounding jubilee;
Arise, Defender! for thy way is clear
And all thy country's heart goes out to thee.

The Story of a Daughter's Love

Aaron Burr was past-master of what Whistler calls "the gentle art of making enemies!" Probably no man ever lived who was more bitterly hated or more fiercely reviled. Even at this day, when he has been dead more than half a century, his memory is still assailed.

It is the popular impression that he was a villain. Perhaps he was, since "where there is smoke, there must be fire," but happily we have no concern with the political part of his life. Whatever he may have been, and whatever dark deeds he may have done, there still remains a redeeming feature which no one has denied him—his love for his daughter, Theodosia.

One must remember that before Burr was two years old, his father, mother, and grandparents were all dead. He was reared by an uncle, Timothy Edwards, who doubtless did his best, but the odds were against the homeless child. Neither must we forget that he fought in the Revolution, bravely and well.

From his early years he was very attractive to women. He was handsome, distinguished, well dressed, and gifted in many ways. He was generous, ready at compliments and gallantry, and possessed an all-compelling charm.

In the autumn of 1777, his regiment was detailed for scouting duty in New Jersey, which was then the debatable ground between colonial and British armies. In January of 1779, Colonel Burr was given command of the "lines" in Westchester County, New York. It was at this time that he first met Mrs. Prevost, the widow of a British officer. She lived across the Hudson, some fifteen miles from shore, and the river was patrolled by the gunboats of the British, and the land by their sentries.

In spite of these difficulties, however, Burr managed to make two calls upon the lady, although they were both necessarily informal. He sent six of his trusted soldiers to a place on the Hudson, where there was an overhanging bank under which they moored a large boat, well supplied with blankets and buffalo robes. At nine o'clock in the evening he left White Plains on the smallest and swiftest horse he could procure, and when he reached the rendezvous, the horse was quickly bound and laid in the boat. Burr and the six troopers stepped in, and in half an hour they were across the ferry. The horse was lifted out, and unbound, and with a little rubbing he was again ready for duty.

Before midnight, Burr was at the house of his beloved, and at four in the morning he came back to the troopers awaiting him on the river bank, and the return trip was made in the same manner.

For a year and a half after leaving the army, Burr was an invalid, but in July, 1782, he married Mrs. Prevost. She was a widow with two sons, and was ten years older than her husband. Her health was delicate and she had a scar on her forehead, but her mind was finely cultivated and her manners charming.

Long after her death he said that if his manners were more graceful than those of some men, it was due to her influence, and that his wife was the truest woman, and most charming lady he had ever known.

It has been claimed by some that Burr's married life was not a happy one, but there are many letters still extant which passed between them which seemed to prove the contrary. Before marriage he did not often write to her, but during his absences afterward, the fondest wife could have no reason to complain.

For instance:

"This morning came your truly welcome letter of Monday evening," he wrote her at one time. "Where did it loiter so long?

"Nothing in my absence is so flattering to me as your health and cheerfulness. I then contemplate nothing so eagerly as my return, amuse myself with ideas of my own happiness, and dwell upon the sweet domestic joys which I fancy prepared for me.

"Nothing is so unfriendly to every species of enjoyment as melancholy. Gloom, however dressed, however caused, is incompatible with friendship. They cannot have place in the mind at the same time. It is the secret, the malignant foe of sentiment and love."

He always wrote fondly of the children:

"My love to the smiling little girl," he said in one letter. "I continually plan my return with childish impatience, and fancy a thousand incidents which are most interesting."

After five years of married life the wife wrote him as follows:

"Your letters always afford me a singular satisfaction, a sensation entirely my own. This was peculiarly so. It wrought strangely upon my mind and spirits. My Aaron, it was replete with tenderness and with the most lively affection. I read and re-read till afraid I should get it by rote, and mingle it with common ideas."

Soon after Burr entered politics, his wife developed cancer of the most virulent character. Everything that money or available skill could accomplish was done for her, but she died after a lingering and painful illness, in the spring of 1794.

They had lived together happily for twelve years, and he grieved for her deeply and sincerely. Yet the greatest and most absorbing passion of his life was for his daughter, Theodosia, who was named for her mother and was born in the first year of their marriage. When little Theodosia was first laid in her father's arms, all that was best in him answered to her mute plea for his affection, and later, all that was best in him responded to her baby smile.

Between those two, there was ever the fullest confidence, never tarnished by doubt or mistrust, and when all the world forsook him, Theodosia, grown to womanhood, stood proudly by her father's side and shared his blame as if it had been the highest honour.

When she was a year or two old, they moved to a large house at the corner of Cedar and Nassau Streets, in New York City. A large garden surrounded it and there were grapevines in the rear. Here the child grew strong and healthy, and laid the foundations of her girlish beauty and mature charm. When she was but three years old her mother wrote to the father, saying:

"Your dear little Theodosia cannot hear you spoken of without an apparent melancholy; insomuch, that her nurse is obliged to exert her invention to divert her, and myself avoid the mention of you in her presence. She was one whole day indifferent to everything but your name. Her attachment is not of a common nature."

And again:

"Your dear little daughter seeks you twenty times a day, calls you to your meals, and will not suffer your chair to be filled by any of the family."

The child was educated as if she had been a boy. She learned to read Latin and Greek fluently, and the accomplishments of her time were not neglected. When she was at school, the father wrote her regularly, and did not allow one of her letters to wait a day for its affectionate answer. He corrected her spelling and her grammar, instilled sound truths into her mind, and formed her habits. From this plastic clay, with inexpressible love and patient toil, he shaped his ideal woman.

She grew into a beautiful girl. Her features were much like her father's. She was petite, graceful, plump, rosy, dignified, and gracious. In her manner, there was a calm assurance—the air of mastery over all situations—which she doubtless inherited from him.

When she was eighteen years of age, she married Joseph Alston of South Carolina, and, with much pain at parting from her father, she went there to live, after seeing him inaugurated as Jefferson's Vice-President. His only consolation was her happiness, and when he returned to New York, he wrote her that he approached the old house as if it had been the sepulchre of all his friends. "Dreary, solitary, comfortless—it was no longer home."

After her mother's death, Theodosia had been the lady of his household and reigned at the head of his table. When he went back there was no loved face opposite him, and the chill and loneliness struck him to the heart.

For three years after her marriage, Theodosia was blissfully happy. A boy was born to her, and was named Aaron Burr Alston. The Vice-President visited them in the South and took his namesake unreservedly into his heart. "If I can see without prejudice," he said, "there never was a finer boy."

His last act before fighting the duel with Hamilton, was writing to his daughter—a happy, gay, care-free letter, giving no hint of what was impending. To her husband he wrote in a different strain, begging him to keep the event from her as long as possible, to make her happy always, and to encourage her in those habits of study which he himself had taught her.

She had parted from him with no other pain in her heart than the approaching separation. When they met again, he was a fugitive from justice, travel-stained from his long journey in an open canoe, indicted for murder in New York, and in New Jersey, although still President of the Senate, and Vice-President of the United States.

The girl's heart ached bitterly, yet no word of censure escaped her lips, and she still held her head high. When his Mexican scheme was overthrown, Theodosia sat beside him at his trial, wearing her absolute faith, so that all the world might see.

When he was preparing for his flight to Europe, Theodosia was in New York, and they met by night, secretly, at the house of friends. Just before he sailed, they spent a whole night together, making the best of the little time that remained to them before the inevitable separation. Early in June they parted, little dreaming that they should see each other no more.

During the years of exile, Theodosia suffered no less than he. Mr. Alston had lost his faith in Aaron Burr, and the woman's heart strained beneath the burden. Her health failed, her friends shrank from her, yet openly and bravely she clung to her father.

Public opinion showed no signs of relenting, and his evil genius followed him across the sea. He was expelled from England, and in Paris he was almost a prisoner. At one time he was obliged to live upon potatoes and dry bread, and his devoted daughter could not help him.

He was despised by his countrymen, but Theodosia's adoring love never faltered. In one of her letters she said:

"I witness your extraordinary fortitude with new wonder at every misfortune. Often, after reflecting on this subject, you appear to me so superior, so elevated above other men—I contemplate you with such a strange mixture of humility, admiration, reverence, love, and pride, that a very little superstition would be necessary to make me worship you as a superior being, such enthusiasm does your character excite in me.

"When I afterward revert to myself, how insignificant do my best qualities appear! My own vanity would be greater if I had not been placed so near you, and yet, my pride is in our relationship. I had rather not live than not to be the daughter of such a man."

She wrote to Mrs. Madison and asked her to intercede with the President for her father. The answer gave the required assurance, and she wrote to her father, urging him to go boldly to New York and resume the practice of his profession. "If worse comes to worst," she wrote, "I will leave everything to suffer with you."

He landed in Boston and went on to New York in May of 1812, where his reception was better than he had hoped, and where he soon had a lucrative practice. They planned for him to come South in the summer, and she was almost happy again, when her child died and her mother's heart was broken.

She had borne much, and she never recovered from that last blow. Her health failed rapidly, and though she was too weak to undertake the trip, she insisted upon going to New York to see her father.

Thinking the voyage might prove beneficial, her husband reluctantly consented, and passage was engaged for her on a pilot-boat that had been out privateering, and had stopped for supplies before going on to New York.

The vessel sailed—and a storm swept the Atlantic coast from Maine to Florida. It was supposed that the ship went down off Cape Hatteras, but forty years afterward, a sailor, who died in Texas, confessed on his death-bed that he was one of a crew of mutineers who took possession of the *Patriot* and forced the passengers, as well as the officers and men, to walk the plank. He professed to remember Mrs. Alston well, and said she was the last one who perished. He never forgot her look of despair as she stepped into the sea—with her head held high even in the face of death.

Among Theodosia's papers was found a letter addressed to her husband, written at a time when she was weary of the struggle. On the envelope was written: "My Husband. To be delivered after my death. I wish this to be read immediately and before my burial."

He never saw the letter, for he never had the courage to go through her papers, and after his death it was sent to her father. It came to him like a message from the grave:

"Let my father see my son, sometimes," she had written. "Do not be unkind to him whom I have loved so much, I beseech of you. Burn all my papers except my father's letters, which I beg you to return to him."

A long time afterward, her father married Madame Jumel, a rich New York woman who was many years his junior, but the alliance was unfortunate, and was soon annulled. Through all the rest of his life, he never wholly gave up the hope that Theodosia might return. He clung fondly to the belief that she had been picked up by another ship, and some day would be brought back to him.

Day by day, he haunted the Battery, anxiously searching the faces of the incoming passengers, asking some of them for tidings of his daughter, and always believing that the next ship would bring her back.

He became a familiar figure, for he was almost always there—a bent, shrunken little man, white-haired, leaning heavily upon his cane, asking questions in a thin piping voice, and straining his dim eyes forever toward the unsounded waters, from whence the idol of his heart never came.

For out within those waters, cruel, changeless,
She sleeps, beyond all rage of earth or sea;
A smile upon her dear lips, dumb, but waiting,
And I—I hear the sea-voice calling me.

The Sea-Voice

Beyond the sands I hear the sea-voice calling
With passion all but human in its pain,
While from my eyes the bitter tears are falling,
And all the summer land seems blind with rain;
For out within those waters, cruel, changeless,
She sleeps, beyond all rage of earth or sea,
A smile upon her dear lips, dumb, but waiting,
And I—I hear the sea-voice calling me.

The tide comes in. The moonlight flood and glory
Of that unresting surge thrill earth with bliss,
And I can hear the passionate sweet story
Of waves that waited round her for her kiss.
Sweetheart, they love you; silent and unseeing,
Old Ocean holds his court around you there,
And while I reach out through the dark to find you
His fingers twine the sea-weed in your hair.

The tide goes out and in the dawn's new splendour
The dreams of dark first fade, then pass away,
And I awake from visions soft and tender
To face the shuddering agony of day
For out within those waters, cruel, changeless,
She sleeps, beyond all rage of earth or sea;
A smile upon her dear lips, dumb, but waiting,
And I—I hear the sea-voice calling me.

The Mystery of Randolph's Courtship

It is said that in order to know a man, one must begin with his ancestors, and the truth of the saying is strikingly exemplified in the case of "John Randolph of Roanoke," as he loved to write his name.

His contemporaries have told us what manner of man he was—fiery, excitable, of strong passions and strong will, capable of great bitterness, obstinate, revengeful, and extremely sensitive.

"I have been all my life," he says, "the creature of impulse, the sport of chance, the victim of my own uncontrolled and uncontrollable sensations, and of a poetic temperament."

He was sarcastic to a degree, proud, haughty, and subject to fits of Byronic despair and morbid gloom. For these traits we must look back to the Norman Conquest from which he traced his descent in an unbroken line, while, on the side of his maternal grandmother, he was the seventh in descent from Pocahontas, the Indian maiden who married John Rolfe.

The Indian blood was evident, even in his personal appearance. He was tall, slender, and dignified in his bearing; his hands were thin, his fingers long and bony; his face was dark, sallow, and wrinkled, oval in shape and seamed with lines by the inward conflict which forever raged in his soul. His chin was pointed but firm, and his lips were set; around his mouth were marked the tiny, almost imperceptible lines which mean cruelty. His nose was aquiline, his ears large at the top, tapering almost to a point at the lobe, and his forehead unusually high and broad. His hair was soft, and his skin, although dark, suffered from extreme sensitiveness.

"There is no accounting for thinness of skins in different animals, human, or brute [he once said]. Mine, I believe to be more tender than many infants of a month old. Indeed I have remarked in myself, from my earliest recollection, a delicacy or effeminacy of complexion, which but for a spice of the devil in my temper would have consigned me to the distaff or the needle."

"A spice of the devil" is mild indeed, considering that before he was four years old he frequently swooned in fits of passion, and was restored to consciousness with difficulty.

His most striking feature was his eyes. They were deep, dark, and fiery, filled with passion and great sadness at the same time. "When he first entered an assembly of people," said one who knew him, "they were the eyes of the eagle in search of his prey, darting about from place to place to see upon whom to light. When he was assailed they flashed fire and proclaimed a torrent of rage within."

The voice of this great statesman was a rare gift:

"One might live a hundred years [says one,] and never hear another like it. The wonder was why the sweet tone of a woman was so harmoniously blended with that of a man. His very whisper could be distinguished above the ordinary tones of other men. His voice was so singularly clear, distinct, and melodious that it was a positive pleasure to hear him articulate anything."

Such was the man who swayed the multitude at will, punished offenders with sarcasm and invective, inspired fear even in his equals, and loved and suffered more than any other prominent man of his generation.

He had many acquaintances, a few friends, and three loves—his mother, his brother, and the beautiful young woman who held his heart in the hollow of her hand, until the Gray Angel, taking pity, closed his eyes in the last sleep.

His mother, who was Frances Bland, married John Randolph in 1769, and John Randolph, of Roanoke, was their third son.

Tradition tells us of the unusual beauty of the mother—

"the high expanded forehead, the smooth arched brow; the brilliant dark eyes; the well defined nose; the full round laughing lips; the tall graceful figure, the beautiful dark hair; an open cheerful countenance—suffused with that deep, rich Oriental tint which never seems to fade, all of which made her the most beautiful and attractive woman of her age."

She was a wife at sixteen, and at twenty-six a widow. Three years after the death of her husband, she married St. George Tucker, of Bermuda who proved to be a kind father to her children.

In the winter of 1781, Benedict Arnold, the traitor who had spread ruin through his native state, was sent to Virginia on an expedition of ravage. He landed at the mouth of the James, and advanced toward Petersburg. Matoax, Randolph's home, was directly in the line of the invading army, so the family set out on a cold January morning, and at night entered the home of Benjamin Ward, Jr.

John Randolph was seven years old, and little Maria Ward had just passed her fifth birthday. The two children played together happily, and in the boy's heart was sown the seed of that grand passion which dominated his life.

After a few days, the family went on to Bizarre, a large estate on both sides of the Appomattox, and here Mrs. Tucker and her sons spent the remainder of the year, while her husband joined General Greene's army, and afterward, the force of Lafayette.

In 1788, John Randolph's mother died, and his first grief swept over him in an overwhelming torrent. The boy of fifteen spent bitter nights, his face buried in the grass, sobbing over his mother's grave. Years afterward, he wrote to a friend, "I am a fatalist. I am all but friendless. Only one human being ever knew me. *She* only knew me."

He kept his mother's portrait always in his room, and enshrined her in loving remembrance in his heart. He had never seen his father's face to remember it distinctly, and for a long time he wore his miniature in his bosom. In 1796, his brother Richard died, and the unexpected blow crushed him to earth. More than thirty years afterward he wrote to his half-brother, Henry St. George Tucker, the following note:

"DEAR HENRY

"Our poor brother Richard was born in 1770. He would have been fifty-six years old the ninth of this month. I can no more.

"J. R. OF R."

At some time in his early manhood he came into close relationship with Maria Ward. She had been an attractive child, and had grown into a woman so beautiful that Lafayette said her equal could not be found in North America. Her hair was auburn, and hung in curls around her face; her skin was exquisitely fair; her eyes were dark and eloquent. Her mouth was well formed; she was slender, graceful, and coquettish, well-educated, and in every way, charming.

To this woman, John Randolph's heart went out in passionate, adoring love. He might be bitter and sarcastic with others, but with her he was gentleness itself. Others might know him as a man of affairs, keen and logical, but to her he was only a lover.

Timid and hesitating at first, afraid perhaps of his fiery wooing, Miss Ward kept him for some time in suspense. All the treasures of his mind and soul were laid before her; that deep, eloquent voice which moved the multitude to tears at its master's will was pleading with a woman for her love.

What wonder that she yielded at last and promised to marry him? Then for a time everything else was forgotten. The world lay before him to be conquered when he might choose. Nothing would be too great for him to accomplish—nothing impossible to that eager joyous soul enthroned at last upon the greatest heights of human happiness. And then—there was a change. He rode to her home one day, tying his horse outside as was his wont. A little later he strode out, shaking like an aspen, his face white in agony. He drew his knife from his pocket, cut the bridle of his horse, dug his spurs into the quivering sides, and was off like the wind. What battle was fought out on that wild ride is known only to John Randolph and his God. What torture that fiery soul went through, no human being can ever know. When he came back at night, he was so changed that no one dared to speak to him.

He threw himself into the political arena in order to save his reason. Often at midnight, he would rise from his uneasy bed, buckle on his pistols, and ride like mad over the country, returning only when his horse was spent. He never saw Miss Ward again, and she married Peyton Randolph, the son of Edmund Randolph, who was Secretary of State under Washington.

The entire affair is shrouded in mystery. There is not a letter, nor a single scrap of paper, nor a shred of evidence upon which to base even a presumption. The separation was final and complete, and the white-hot metal of the man's nature was gradually moulded into that strange eccentric being whose foibles are so well known.

Only once did Randolph lift even a corner of the veil. In a letter to his dearest friend he spoke of her as:

"One I loved better than my own soul, or Him who created it. My apathy is not natural, but superinduced. There was a volcano under my ice, but it burnt out, and a face of desolation has come on, not to be rectified in ages, could my life be prolonged to patriarchal longevity.

"The necessity of loving and being loved was never felt by the imaginary beings of Rousseau and Byron's creation, more imperiously than by myself. My heart was offered with a devotion that knew no reserve. Long an object of proscription and treachery, I have at last, more mortifying to the pride of man, become an object of utter indifference."

The brilliant statesman would doubtless have had a large liberty of choice among the many beautiful women of his circle, but he never married, and there is no record of any entanglement. To the few women he deemed worthy of his respect and admiration, he was deferential and even gallant. In one of his letters to a young relative he said:

"Love to god-son Randolph and respectful compliments to Mrs. R. She is indeed a fine woman, one for whom I have felt a true regard, unmixed with the foible of another passion.

"Fortunately or unfortunately for me, when I knew her, I bore a charmed heart. Nothing else could have preserved me from the full force of her attractions."

For much of the time after his disappointment, he lived alone with his servants, solaced as far as possible by those friends of all mankind—books. When the spirit moved him, he would make visits to the neighbouring plantations, sometimes dressed in white flannel trousers, coat, and vest, and with white paper wrapped around his beaver hat! When he presented himself in this manner, riding horseback, with his dark eyes burning, he was said to have presented "a most ghostly appearance!"

An old lady who lived for years on the banks of the Staunton, near Randolph's solitary home, tells a pathetic story:

She was sitting alone in her room in the dead of winter, when a beautiful woman, pale as a ghost, dressed entirely in white, suddenly appeared before her, and began to talk about Mr. Randolph, saying he was her lover and would marry her yet, as he had never proved false to his plighted faith. She talked of him incessantly, like one deranged, until a young gentleman came by the house, leading a horse with a side-saddle on. She rushed out, and asked his permission to ride a few miles. Greatly to his surprise, she mounted without assistance, and sat astride like a man. He was much embarrassed, but had no choice except to escort her to the end of her journey.

The old lady who tells of this strange experience says that the young woman several times visited Mr. Randolph, always dressed in white and usually in the dead of winter. He always put her on a horse and sent her away with a servant to escort her.

In his life there were but two women—his mother and Maria Ward. While his lips were closed on the subject of his love, he did not hesitate to avow his misery. "I too am wretched," he would say with infinite pathos; and after her death, he spoke of Maria Ward as his "angel."

In a letter written sometime after she died, he said, strangely enough: "I loved, aye, and was loved again, not wisely, but too well."

His brilliant career was closed when he was sixty years old, and in his last illness, during delirium, the name of Maria was frequently heard by those who were anxiously watching with him. But, true to himself and to her, even when his reason was dethroned, he said nothing more.

He was buried on his own plantation, in the midst of "that boundless contiguity of shade," with his secret locked forever in his tortured breast. "John Randolph of Roanoke," was all the title he claimed; but the history of those times teaches us that he was more than that—he was John Randolph, of the Republic.

How President Jackson Won His Wife

In October of 1788, a little company of immigrants arrived in Tennessee. The star of empire, which is said to move westward, had not yet illumined Nashville, and it was one of the dangerous points "on the frontier."

The settlement was surrounded on all sides by hostile Indians. Men worked in the fields, but dared not go out to their daily task without being heavily armed. When two men met, and stopped for a moment to talk, they often stood back to back, with their rifles cocked ready for instant use. No one stooped to drink from a spring unless another guarded him, and the women were always attended by an armed force.

Col. John Donelson had built for himself a blockhouse of unusual size and strength, and furnished it comfortably; but while surveying a piece of land near the village, he was killed by the savages, and his widow left to support herself as best she could.

A married daughter and her husband lived with her, but it was necessary for her to take other boarders. One day there was a vigorous rap upon the stout door of the blockhouse, and a young man whose name was Andrew Jackson was admitted. Shortly afterward, he took up his abode as a regular boarder at the Widow Donelson's.

The future President was then twenty-one or twenty-two. He was tall and slender, with every muscle developed to its utmost strength. He had an attractive face, pleasing manners, and made himself agreeable to every one in the house.

The dangers of the frontier were but minor incidents in his estimation, for "desperate courage makes one a majority," and he had courage. When he was but thirteen years of age, he had boldly defied a British officer who had ordered him to clean some cavalry boots.

"Sir," said the boy, "I am a prisoner of war, and I claim to be treated as such!"

With an oath the officer drew his sword, and struck at the child's head. He parried the blow with his left arm, but received a severe wound on his head and another on his arm, the scars of which he always carried.

The protecting presence of such a man was welcome to those who dwelt in the blockhouse—Mrs. Donelson, Mr. and Mrs. Robards, and another boarder, John Overton. Mrs. Donelson was a good cook and a notable housekeeper, while her daughter was said to be "the best story teller, the best dancer, the sprightliest companion, and the most dashing horsewoman in the western country."

Jackson, as the only licensed lawyer in that part of Tennessee, soon had plenty of business on his hands, and his life in the blockhouse was a happy one until he learned that the serpent of jealousy lurked by that fireside.

Mrs. Robards was a comely brunette, and her dusky beauty carried with it an irresistible appeal. Jackson soon learned that Captain Robards was unreasonably and even insanely jealous of his wife, and he learned from John Overton that before his arrival there had been a great deal of unhappiness because of this.

At one time Captain Robards had written to Mrs. Donelson to take her daughter home, as he did not wish to live with her any longer; but through the efforts of Mr. Overton a reconciliation had been effected between the pair, and they were still living together at Mrs. Donelson's when Jackson went there to board.

In a short time, however, Robards became violently jealous of Jackson and talked abusively to his wife, even in the presence of her mother and amidst the tears of both. Once more Overton interfered, assured Robards that his suspicions were groundless, and reproached him for his unmanly conduct.

It was all in vain, however, and the family was in as unhappy a state as before, when they were living with the Captain's mother who had always taken the part of her daughter-in-law.

At length Overton spoke to Jackson about it, telling him it was better not to remain where his presence made so much trouble, and offered to go with him to another boarding-place. Jackson readily assented, though neither of them knew where to go, and said that he would talk to Captain Robards.

The men met near the orchard fence, and Jackson remonstrated with the Captain who grew violently angry and threatened to strike him. Jackson told him that he would not advise him to try to fight, but if he insisted, he would try to give him satisfaction. Nothing came of the discussion, however, as Robards seemed willing to take Jackson's advice and did not dare to strike him. But the coward continued to abuse his wife, and insulted Jackson at every opportunity. The result was that the young lawyer left the house.

A few months later, the still raging husband left his wife and went to Kentucky, which was then a part of Virginia. Soon afterward, Mrs. Robards went to live with her sister, Mrs. Hay, and Overton returned to Mrs. Donelson's.

In the following autumn there was a rumour that Captain Robards intended to return to Tennessee and take his wife to Kentucky, at which Mrs. Donelson and her daughter were greatly distressed. Mrs. Robards wept bitterly, and said it was impossible for her to live peaceably with her husband as she had tried it twice and failed. She determined to go down the river to Natchez, to a friend, and thus avoid her husband, who she said had threatened to haunt her.

When Jackson heard of this arrangement he was very much troubled, for he felt that he had been the unwilling cause of the young wife's unhappiness, although entirely innocent of any wrong intention. So when Mrs. Robards had fully determined to undertake the journey to Natchez, accompanied only by Colonel Stark and his family, he offered to go with them as an additional protection against the Indians who were then especially active, and his escort was very gladly accepted. The trip was made in safety, and after seeing the lady settled with her friends, he returned to Nashville and resumed his law practice.

At that time there was no divorce law in Virginia, and each separate divorce required the passage of an act of the legislature before a jury could consider the case. In the winter of 1791, Captain Robards obtained the passage of such an act, authorising the court of Mercer County to act upon his divorce. Mrs. Robards, hearing of this, understood that the passage of the act was, in itself, divorce, and that she was a free woman. Jackson also took the divorce for granted. Every one in the country so understood the matter, and at Natchez, in the following summer, the two were married.

They returned to Nashville, settled down, and Jackson began in earnest the career that was to land him in the White House, the hero of the nation.

In December of 1793, more than two years after their marriage, their friend Overton learned that the legislature had not granted a divorce, but had left it for the court to do so. Jackson was much chagrined when he heard of this, and it was with great difficulty that he was brought to believe it. In January of 1794, when the decree was finally obtained, they were married again.

It is difficult to excuse Jackson for marrying the woman without positive and absolute knowledge of her divorce. He was a lawyer, and could have learned the facts of the case, even though there was no established mail service. Each of them had been entirely innocent of any intentional wrong-doing, and their long life together, their great devotion to each other, and General Jackson's honourable career, forever silenced the spiteful calumny of his rivals and enemies of early life.

In his eyes his wife was the soul of honour and purity; he loved and reverenced her as a man loves and reverences but one woman in his lifetime, and for thirty-seven years he kept a pair of pistols loaded for the man who should dare to breathe her name without respect.

The famous pistol duel with Dickinson was the result of a quarrel which had its beginning in a remark reflecting upon Mrs. Jackson, and Dickinson, though a crack shot, paid for it with his life.

Several of Dickinson's friends sent a memorial to the proprietors of the *Impartial Review*, asking that the next number of the paper appear in mourning, "out of respect for the memory, and regret for the untimely death, of Mr. Charles Dickinson."

"Old Hickory" heard of this movement, and wrote to the proprietors, asking that the names of the gentlemen making the request be published in the memorial number of the paper. This also was agreed to, and it is significant that twenty-six of the seventy-three men who had signed the petition called and erased their names from the document.

"The Hermitage" at Nashville, which is still a very attractive spot for visitors, was built solely to please Mrs. Jackson, and there she dispensed gracious hospitality. Not merely a guest or two, but whole families, came for weeks at a time, for the mistress of the mansion was fond of entertaining, and proved herself a charming hostess. She had a good memory, had passed through many and greatly varied experiences, and above all she had that rare faculty which is called tact.

Though her husband's love for her was evident to every one, yet, in the presence of others, he always maintained a dignified reserve. He never spoke of her as "Rachel," nor addressed her as "My Dear." It was always "Mrs. Jackson," or "wife." She always called him "Mr. Jackson," never "Andrew" nor "General."

Both of them greatly desired children, but this blessing was denied them; so they adopted a boy, the child of Mrs. Jackson's brother, naming him "Andrew Jackson," and bringing him up as their own child.

The lady's portrait shows her to have been wonderfully attractive. It does not reveal the dusky Oriental tint of her skin, the ripe red of her lips, nor the changing lights in her face, but it shows the high forehead, the dark soft hair, the fine eyes, and the tempting mouth which was smiling, yet serene. A lace head-dress is worn over the waving hair, and the filmy folds fall softly over neck and bosom.

When Jackson was elected to the Presidency, the ladies of Nashville organized themselves into sewing circles to prepare Mrs. Jackson's wardrobe. It was a labour of love. On December 23, 1828, there was to be a grand banquet in Jackson's honour, and the devoted women of their home city had made a beautiful gown for his wife to wear at the dinner. At sunrise the preparations began. The tables were set, the dining-room decorated, and the officers and men of the troop that was to escort the President-elect were preparing to go to the home and attend him on the long ride into the city. Their horses were saddled and in readiness at the place of meeting. As the bugle sounded the summons to mount, a breathless messenger appeared on a horse flecked with foam. Mrs. Jackson had died of heart disease the evening before.

The festival was changed to a funeral, and the trumpets and drums that were to have sounded salute were muffled in black. All decorations were taken down, and the church bells tolled mournfully. The grief of the people was beyond speech. Each one felt a personal loss.

At the home the blow was terrible. The lover-husband would not leave his wife. In those bitter hours the highest gift of his countrymen was an empty triumph, for his soul was wrecked with the greatness of his loss.

When she was buried at the foot of a slope in the garden of "The Hermitage," his bereavement came home to him with crushing strength. Back of the open grave stood a great throng of people, waiting in the wintry wind. The sun shone brightly on the snow, but "The Hermitage" was desolate, for its light and laughter and love were gone. The casket was carried down the slope, and a long way behind it came the General, slowly and almost helpless, between two of his friends.

The people of Nashville had made ready to greet him with the blare of bugles, waving flags, the clash of cymbals, and resounding cheers. It was for the President-elect—the hero of the war. The throng that stood behind the open grave greeted him with sobs and tears—not the President-elect, but the man bowed by his sixty years, bareheaded, with his gray hair rumpled in the wind, staggering toward them in the throes of his bitterest grief.

In that one night he had grown old. He looked like a man stricken beyond all hope. When his old friends gathered around him with the tears streaming down their cheeks, wringing his hand in silent sympathy, he could make no response.

He was never the same again, though his strength of will and his desperate courage fought with this infinite pain. For the rest of his life he lived as she would have had him live—guided his actions by the thought of what his wife, if living, would have had him do—loving her still, with the love that passeth all understanding.

He declined the sarcophagus fit for an emperor, that he might be buried like a simple citizen, in the garden by her side.

His last words were of her—his last look rested upon her portrait that hung opposite his bed, and if there be dreaming in the dark, the vision of her brought him peace at last.

The Bachelor President's Loyalty
to a Memory

The fifteenth President was remarkable among the men of his time for his lifelong fidelity to one woman, for since the days of knight-errantry such devotion has been as rare as it is beautiful. The young lawyer came of Scotch-Irish parentage, and to this blending of blood were probably in part due his deep love and steadfastness. There was rather more of the Irish than of the Scotch in his face, and when we read that his overflowing spirits were too much for the college in which he had been placed, and that, for "reasons of public policy," the honours which he had earned were on commencement day given to another, it is evident that he may sometimes have felt that he owed allegiance primarily to the Emerald Isle.

Like others, who have been capable of deep and lasting passion, James Buchanan loved his mother. Among his papers there was found a fragment of an autobiography, which ended in 1816, when the writer was only twenty-five years of age. He says his father was "a kind father, a sincere friend, and an honest and religious man," but on the subject of his mother he waxes eloquent:

"Considering her limited opportunities in early life [he writes], my mother was a remarkable woman. The daughter of a country farmer, engaged in household employment from early life until after my father's death, she yet found time to read much, and to reflect deeply on what she read.

"She had a great fondness for poetry, and could repeat with ease all the passages in her favorite authors which struck her fancy. These were Milton, Pope, Young, Cowper, and Thompson.

"I do not think, at least until a late period in life, she had ever read a criticism on any one of these authors, and yet such was the correctness of her natural taste, that she had selected for herself, and could repeat, every passage in them which has been admired....

"For her sons, as they grew up successively, she was a delightful and instructive companion.... She was a woman of great firmness of character, and bore the afflictions of her later life with Christian philosophy.... It was chiefly to her influence, that her sons were indebted for a liberal education. Under Providence I attribute any little distinction which I may have acquired in the world to the blessing which He conferred upon me in granting me such a mother."

If Elizabeth Buchanan could have read these words, doubtless she would have felt fully repaid for her many years of toil, self-sacrifice, and devotion.

After the young man left the legislature and took up the practice of law, with the intention of spending his life at the bar, he became engaged to Anne Coleman, the daughter of Robert Coleman, of Lancaster.

She is said to have been an unusually beautiful girl, quiet, gentle, modest, womanly, and extremely sensitive. The fine feelings of a delicately organized nature may easily become either a blessing or a curse, and on account of her sensitiveness there was a rupture for which neither can be very greatly blamed.

Mr. Coleman approved of the engagement, and the happy lover worked hard to make a home for the idol of his heart. One day, out of the blue sky a thunderbolt fell. He received a note from Miss Coleman asking him to release her from her engagement.

There was no explanation forthcoming, and it was not until long afterward that he discovered that busy-bodies and gossips had gone to Miss Coleman with stories concerning him which had no foundation save in their mischief-making imaginations, and which she would not repeat to him. After all his efforts at re-establishing the old relations had proved useless, he wrote to her that if it were her wish to be released from her engagement he could but submit, as he had no desire to hold her against her will.

The break came in the latter part of the summer of 1819, when he was twenty-eight years old and she was in her twenty-third year. He threw himself into his work with renewed energy, and later on she went to visit friends in Philadelphia.

Though she was too proud to admit it, there was evidence that the beautiful and high-spirited girl was suffering from heartache. On the ninth of December, she died suddenly, and her body was brought home just a week after she left Lancaster. The funeral took place the next day, Sunday, and to the suffering father of the girl, the heart-broken lover wrote a letter which in simple pathos stands almost alone. It is the only document on this subject which remains, but in these few lines is hidden a tragedy:

"LANCASTER, December 10, 1819.

"MY DEAR SIR:

"You have lost a child, a dear, dear child. I have lost the only earthly object of my affections, without whom, life now presents to me a dreary blank. My prospects are all cut off, and I feel that my happiness will be buried with her in her grave.

"It is now no time for explanation, but the time will come when you will discover that she, as well as I, has been greatly abused. God forgive the authors of it! My feelings of resentment against them, whoever they may be, are buried in the dust.

"I have now one request to make, and for the love of God, and of your dear departed daughter, whom I loved infinitely more than any human being could love, deny me not. Afford me the melancholy pleasure of seeing her body before its interment. I would not, for the world, be denied this request.

"I might make another, but from the misrepresentations that have been made to you, I am almost afraid. I would like to follow her remains, to the grave as a mourner. I would like to convince the world, I hope yet to convince you, that she was infinitely dearer to me than life.

"I may sustain the shock of her death, but I feel that happiness has fled from me forever. The prayer which I make to God without ceasing is, that I yet may be able to show my veneration for the memory of my dear, departed saint, by my respect and attachment for her surviving friends.

"May Heaven bless you and enable you to bear the shock with the fortitude of a Christian.

"I am forever, your sincere and grateful friend,

"JAMES BUCHANAN."

The father returned the letter unopened and without comment. Death had only widened the breach. It would have been gratifying to know that the two lovers were together for a moment at the end.

For such a meeting as that there are no words but Edwin Arnold's:

"But he—who loved her too well to dread
The sweet, the stately, the beautiful dead—
He lit his lamp, and took the key,
And turn'd it!—alone again—he and she!"

For him there was not even a glimpse of her as she lay in her coffin, nor a whisper that some day, like Evelyn Hope, she might "wake, and remember and understand." With that love that asks only for the right to serve, and feeling perhaps that no pen could do her justice, he obtained permission to write a paragraph for a local paper, which was published unsigned:

"Departed this life, on Thursday morning last, in the twenty-third year of her age, while on a visit to friends in the city of Philadelphia, Miss Anne C. Coleman, daughter of Robert Coleman, Esquire of this city.

"It rarely falls to our lot to shed a tear over the remains of one so much and so deservedly beloved as was the deceased. She was everything which the fondest parent, or the fondest friend could have wished her to be.

"Although she was young and beautiful and accomplished, and the smiles of fortune shone upon her, yet her native modesty and worth made her unconscious of her own attractions. Her heart was the seat of all the softer virtues which ennoble and dignify the character of woman.

"She has now gone to a world, where, in the bosom of her God, she will be happy with congenial spirits. May the memory of her virtues be ever green in the hearts of her surviving friends. May her mild spirit, which on earth still breathes peace and good will, be their guardian angel to preserve them from the faults to which she was ever a stranger.

"The spider's most attenuated thread
Is cord, is cable, to man's tender tie
On earthly bliss—it breaks at every breeze."

How deeply he felt her death is shown by extracts from a letter written to him by a friend in the latter part of December:

"I am writing, I know not why, and perhaps had better not. I write only to speak of the awful visitation of Providence that has fallen upon you, and how deeply I feel it.... I trust to your philosophy and courage, and to the elasticity of spirits natural to most young men....

"The sun will shine again, though a man enveloped in gloom always thinks the darkness is to be eternal. Do you remember the Spanish anecdote?

"A lady who had lost a favorite child remained for months sunk in sullen sorrow and despair. Her confessor, one morning visited her, and found her, as usual immersed in gloom and grief. 'What,' said he, 'Have you not forgiven God Almighty?'

"She rose, exerted herself, joined the world again, and became useful to herself and her friends."

Time's kindly touch heals many wounds, but the years seemed to bring to James Buchanan no surcease of sorrow. He was always under the cloud of that misunderstanding, and during his long political career, the incident frequently served as a butt for the calumnies of his enemies. It was freely used in "campaign documents," perverted, misrepresented, and twisted into every conceivable shape, though it is difficult to conceive how any form of humanity could ever be so base.

Next to the loss of the girl he loved, this was the greatest grief of his life. To see the name of his "dear, departed saint" dragged into newspaper notoriety was absolute torture. Denial was useless, and pleading had no effect. After he had retired to his home at Wheatland, and when he was past seventy—when Anne Coleman's beautiful body had gone back to the dust, there was a long article in a newspaper about the affair, accompanied by the usual misrepresentations.

To a friend, he said, with deep emotion: "In my safety-deposit box in New York there is a sealed package, containing papers and relics which will explain everything. Sometime, when I am dead, the world will know—and absolve."

But after his death, when his executors found the package, there was a direction on the outside: "To be burned unopened at my death."

He chose silence rather than vindication at the risk of having Anne Coleman's name again brought into publicity. In that little parcel there was doubtless full exoneration, but at the end, as always, he nobly bore the blame.

It happened that the letter he had written to her father was not in this package, but among his papers at Wheatland—otherwise that pathetic request would also have been burned.

Through all his life he remained true to Anne's memory. Under the continual public attacks his grief became one that even his friends forebore to speak of, and he had a chivalrous regard for all women, because of his love for one. His social instincts were strong, his nature affectionate and steadfast, yet it was owing to his disappointment that he became President. At one time, when he was in London, he said to an intimate friend: "I never intended to engage in politics, but meant to follow my profession strictly. But my prospects and plans were all changed by a most sad event, which happened at Lancaster when I was a young man. As a distraction from my grief, and because I saw that through a political following I could secure the friends I then needed, I accepted a nomination."

A beautiful side of his character is shown in his devotion to his niece, Harriet Lane. He was to her always a faithful father. When she was away at school or otherwise separated from him, he wrote to her regularly, never failing to assure her of his affection, and received her love and confidence in return. In 1865, when she wrote to him of her engagement, he replied, in part, as follows:

"I believe you say truly that nothing would have induced you to leave me, in good or evil fortune, if I had wished you to remain with me.

"Such a wish on my part would be very selfish. You have long known my desire that you should marry whenever a suitor worthy of you should offer.

Indeed, it has been my strong desire to see you settled in the world before my death. You have now made your own unbiased choice; and from the character of Mr. Johnston, I anticipate for you a happy marriage, because I believe from your own good sense, you will conform to your conductor, and make him a good and loving wife."

The days passed in retirement at Wheatland were filled with quiet content. The end came as peacefully as the night itself. He awoke from a gentle sleep, murmured, "O Lord, God Almighty, as Thou wilt!" and passed serenely into that other sleep, which knows not dreams.

The impenetrable veil between us and eternity permits no lifting of its folds; there is no parting of its greyness, save for a passage, but perhaps, in "that undiscovered country from whose bourne no traveller returns" Anne Coleman and her lover have met once more, and the long life of faithfulness at last has won her pardon.

Decoration Day

The trees bow their heads in sorrow,
While their giant branches wave,
With the requiems of the forest,
To the dead in a soldier's grave.

The pitying rain falls softly,
In grief for a nation's brave,
Who died 'neath the scourge of treason
And rest in a lonely grave.

So, under the willow and cypress
We lay our dead away,
And cover their graves with blossoms,
But the debt we never can pay.

All nature is bathed in tears,
On our sad Memorial day,
When we crown the valour of heroes
With flowers from the garments of May.

The Romance of the Life of Lincoln

By the slow passing of years humanity attains what is called the "historical perspective," but it is still a mooted question as to how many years are necessary.

We think of Lincoln as a great leader, and it is difficult to imagine him as a lover. He was at the helm of "the Ship of State" in the most fearful storm it ever passed through; he struck off the shackles of a fettered people, and was crowned with martyrdom; yet in spite of his greatness, he loved like other men.

There is no record for Lincoln's earlier years of the boyish love which comes to many men in their school days. The great passion of his life came to him in manhood but with no whit of its sweetness gone. Sweet Anne Rutledge! There are those who remember her well, and to this day in speaking of her, their eyes fill with tears. A lady who knew her says: "Miss Rutledge had auburn hair, blue eyes, and a fair complexion. She was pretty, rather slender, and good-hearted, beloved by all who knew her."

Before Lincoln loved her, she had a sad experience with another man. About the time that he came to New Salem, a young man named John McNeil drifted in from one of the Eastern States. He worked hard, was plucky and industrious, and soon accumulated a little property. He met Anne Rutledge when she was but seventeen and still in school, and he began to pay her especial attention which at last culminated in their engagement.

He was about going back to New York for a visit and leaving he told Anne that his name was not McNeil, but McNamar—that he had changed his name so that his dependent family might not follow him and settle down upon him before he was able to support them. Now that he was in a position to aid his parents, brothers, and sisters, he was going back to do it and upon his return would make Anne his wife.

For a long time she did not hear from him at all, and gossip was rife in New Salem. His letters became more formal and less frequent and finally ceased altogether. The girl's proud spirit compelled her to hold her head high amid the impertinent questions of the neighbors.

Lincoln had heard of the strange conduct of McNeil and concluding that there was now no tie between Miss Rutledge and her quondam lover, he began his own siege in earnest. Anne consented at last to marry him provided he gave her time to write to McNamar and obtain a release from the pledge which she felt was still binding upon her.

She wrote, but there was no answer and at last she definitely accepted Lincoln.

It was necessary for him to complete his law studies, and after that, he said, "Nothing on God's footstool shall keep us apart."

He worked happily but a sore conflict seemed to be raging in Anne's tender heart and conscience, and finally the strain told upon her to such an extent that when she was attacked by a fever, she had little strength to resist it.

The summer waned and Anne's life ebbed with it. At the very end of her illness, when all visitors were forbidden, she insisted upon seeing Lincoln. He went to her—and closed the door between them and the world. It was his last hour with her. When he came out, his face was white with the agony of parting.

A few days later, she died and Lincoln was almost insane with grief. He walked for hours in the woods, refused to eat, would speak to no one, and there settled upon him that profound melancholy which came back, time and again, during the after years. To one friend he said: "I cannot bear to think that the rain and storms will beat upon her grave."

When the days were dark and stormy he was constantly watched, as his friends feared he would take his own life. Finally, he was persuaded to go away to the house of a friend who lived at some distance, and here he remained until he was ready to face the world again.

A few weeks after Anne's burial, McNamar returned to New Salem. On his arrival he met Lincoln at the post-office and both were sorely distressed. He made no explanation of his absence, and shortly seemed to forget about Miss Rutledge, but her grave was in Lincoln's heart until the bullet of the assassin struck him down.

In October of 1833, Lincoln met Miss Mary Owens, and admired her though not extravagantly. From all accounts, she was an unusual woman. She was tall, full in figure, with blue eyes and dark hair; she was well educated and quite popular in the little community. She was away for a time, but returned to New Salem in 1836, and Lincoln at once began to call upon her, enjoying her wit and beauty. At that time she was about twenty-eight years old.

One day Miss Owens was out walking with a lady friend and when they came to the foot of a steep hill, Lincoln joined them. He walked behind with Miss Owens, and talked with her, quite oblivious to the fact that her friend was carrying a heavy baby. When they reached the summit, Miss Owens said laughingly: "You would not make a good husband, Abe."

They sat on the fence and a wordy discussion followed. Both were angry when they parted, and the breach was not healed for some time. It was poor policy to quarrel, since some time before he had proposed to Miss Owens, and she had asked for time in which to consider it before giving a final answer. His letters to her are not what one would call "love-letters." One begins in this way:

"MARY:—I have been sick ever since my arrival, or I should have written sooner. It is but little difference, however, as I have very little even yet to write. And more, the longer I can avoid the mortification of looking in the post-office for your letter, and not finding it, the better. You see I am mad about that old letter yet. I don't like very well to risk you again. I'll try you once more, anyhow."

The remainder of the letter deals with political matters and is signed simply "Your Friend Lincoln."

In another letter written the following year he says to her:

"I am often thinking about what we said of your coming to live at Springfield. I am afraid you would not be satisfied. There is a great deal of flourishing about in carriages here, which it would be your doom to see without sharing it. You would have to be poor without the means of hiding your poverty. Do you believe you could bear that patiently?

"Whatever woman may cast her lot with mine, should any ever do so, it is my intention to do all in my power to make her happy and contented; and there is nothing I can imagine that would make me more unhappy than to fail in the effort.

"I know I should be much happier with you than the way I am, provided I saw no signs of discontent in you. What you have said to me may have been in the way of jest, or I may have misunderstood it.

"If so, then let it be forgotten; if otherwise I much wish you would think seriously before you decide. For my part, I have already decided.

"What I have said I will most positively abide by, provided you wish it. My opinion is that you would better not do it. You have not been accustomed to hardship, and it may be more severe than you now imagine.

"I know you are capable of thinking correctly upon any subject and if you deliberate maturely upon this before you decide, then I am willing to abide by your decision."

Matters went on in this way for about three months; then they met again, seemingly without making any progress. On the day they parted, Lincoln wrote her another letter, evidently to make his own position clear and put the burden of decision upon her.

"If you feel yourself in any degree bound to me [he said], I am now willing to release you, provided you wish it; while, on the other hand, I am willing and even anxious, to bind you faster, if I can be convinced that it will in any considerable degree add to your happiness. This, indeed, is the whole question with me. Nothing would make me more miserable than to believe you miserable—nothing more happy than to know you were so."

In spite of his evident sincerity, it is not surprising to learn that a little later, Miss Owens definitely refused him. In April, of the following year, Lincoln wrote to his friend, Mrs. L. H. Browning, giving a full account of this grotesque courtship:

"I finally was forced to give it up [he wrote] at which I very unexpectedly found myself mortified almost beyond endurance.

"I was mortified it seemed to me in a hundred different ways. My vanity was deeply wounded by the reflection that I had so long been too stupid to discover her intentions, and at the same time never doubting that I understood them perfectly; and also, that she, whom I had taught myself to believe nobody else would have, had actually rejected me, with all my fancied greatness.

"And then to cap the whole, I then, for the first time, began to suspect that I was really a little in love with her. But let it all go. I'll try and outlive it. Others have been made fools of by the girls; but this can never with truth be said of me. I most emphatically in this instance made a fool of myself. I have now come to the conclusion never again to think of marrying, and for this reason I can never be satisfied with any one who would be blockhead enough to have me!"

The gist of the matter seems to be that at heart Lincoln hesitated at matrimony, as other men have done, both before and since his time. In his letter to Mrs. Browning he speaks of his efforts to "put off the evil day for a time, which I really dreaded as much, perhaps more, than an Irishman does the halter!"

But in 1839 Miss Mary Todd came to live with her sister, Mrs. Ninian Edwards, at Springfield. She was in her twenty-first year, and is described as "of average height and compactly built." She had a well-rounded face, rich dark brown hair, and bluish grey eyes. No picture of her fails to show the full, well-developed chin, which, more than any other feature is an evidence of determination. She was strong, proud, passionate, gifted with a keen sense of the ridiculous, well educated, and swayed only by her own imperious will.

Lincoln was attracted at once, and strangely enough, Stephen A. Douglas crossed his wooing. For a time the two men were rivals, the pursuit waxing more furious day by day. Some one asked Miss Todd which of them she intended to marry, and she answered laughingly: "The one who has the best chance of becoming President!"

She is said, however, to have refused the "Little Giant" on account of his lax morality and after that the coast was clear for Lincoln. Miss Todd's sister tells us that "he was charmed by Mary's wit and fascinated by her quick sagacity, her will, her nature, and culture." "I have happened in the room," she says, "where they were sitting, often and often, and Mary led the conversation. Lincoln would listen, and gaze on her as if drawn by some superior power— irresistibly so; he listened, but scarcely ever said a word."

The affair naturally culminated in an engagement, and the course of love was running smoothly, when a distracting element appeared in the shape of Miss Matilda Edwards, the sister of Mrs. Edwards's husband. She was young and fair, and Lincoln was pleased with her appearance. For a time he tried to go on as before, but his feelings were too strong to be concealed. Mr. Edwards endeavoured to get his sister to marry Lincoln's friend, Speed, but she refused both Speed and Douglas.

It is said that Lincoln once went to Miss Todd's house, intending to break the engagement, but his real love proved too strong to allow him to do it.

His friend, Speed, thus describes the conclusion of this episode. "Well, old fellow," I said, "did you do as you intended?"

"Yes, I did," responded Lincoln thoughtfully, "and when I told Mary I did not love her, she, wringing her hands, said something about the deceiver being himself deceived."

"What else did you say?"

"To tell you the truth, Speed, it was too much for me. I found the tears trickling down my own cheeks. I caught her in my arms and kissed her."

"And that's how you broke the engagement. Your conduct was tantamount to a renewal of it!"

And indeed this was true, and the lovers again considered the time of marriage.

There is a story by Herndon to the effect that a wedding was arranged for the first day of January, 1841, and then when the hour came Lincoln did not appear, and was found wandering alone in the woods plunged in the deepest melancholy—a melancholy bordering upon insanity.

This story, however, has no foundation; in fact, most competent witnesses agree that no such marriage date was fixed, although some date may have been considered.

It is certain, however, that the relations between Lincoln and Miss Todd were broken off for a time. He did go to Kentucky for a while, but this trip certainly was not due to insanity. Lincoln was never so mindless as some of his biographers would have us believe, and the breaking of the engagement was due to perfectly natural causes—the difference in temperament of the lovers, and Lincoln's inclination to procrastinate. After a time the strained relations gradually improved. They met occasionally in the parlor of a friend, Mrs. Francis, and it was through Miss Todd that the duel with Shields came about.

She wielded a ready and a sarcastic pen, and safely hidden behind a pseudonym and the promise of the editor, she wrote a series of satirical articles for the local paper, entitled: "Letters from Lost Townships." In one of these she touched up Mr. Shields, the Auditor of State, to such good purpose that believing that Lincoln had written the article, he challenged him to a duel. Lincoln accepted the challenge and chose "cavalry broadswords" as the weapons, but the intervention of friends prevented any fighting, although he always spoke of the affair as his "duel."

As a result of this altercation with Shields, Miss Todd and the future President came again into close friendship, and a marriage was decided upon.

The license was secured, the minister sent for, and on November 4, 1842, they became man and wife.

It is not surprising that more or less unhappiness obtained in their married life, for Mrs. Lincoln was a woman of strong character, proud, fiery, and determined. Her husband was subject to strange moods and impulses, and the great task which God had committed to him made him less amenable to family cares.

That married life which began at the Globe Tavern was destined to end at the White House, after years of vicissitude and serious national trouble. Children were born unto them, and all but the eldest died. Great responsibilities were laid upon Lincoln and even though he met them bravely it was inevitable that his family should also suffer.

Upon the face of the Commander-in-chief rested nearly always a mighty sadness, except when it was occasionally illumined by his wonderful smile, or when the light of his sublime faith banished the clouds.

Storm and stress, suffering and heartache, reverses and defeat were the portion of the Leader, and when Victory at last perched upon the National standard, her beautiful feet were all drabbled in blood, and the most terrible war on the world's records passed down into history. In the hour of triumph, with his great purpose nobly fulfilled, death came to the great Captain.

The United Republic is his monument, and that rugged, yet gracious figure, hallowed by martyrdom, stands before the eyes of his countrymen forever serene and calm, while his memory lingers like a benediction in the hearts of both friend and foe.

Silent Thanksgiving

She is standing alone by the window—
A woman, faded and old,
But the wrinkled face was lovely once,
And the silvered hair was gold.
As out in the darkness, the snow-flakes
Are falling so softly and slow,
Her thoughts fly back to the summer of life,
And the scenes of long ago.

Before the dim eyes, a picture comes,
She has seen it again and again;
The tears steal over the faded cheeks,
And the lips that quiver with pain,
For she hears once more the trumpet call
And sees the battle array
As they march to the hills with gleaming swords—
Can she ever forget that day?

She has given her boy to the land she loves,
How hard it had been to part!
And to-night she stands at the window alone,
With a new-made grave in her heart.
And yet, it's the day of Thanksgiving—
But her child, her darling was slain
By the shot and shell of the rebel guns—
Can she ever be thankful again?

She thinks once more of his fair young face,
And the cannon's murderous roll,
While hatred springs in her passionate heart,
And bitterness into her soul.
Then out of the death-like stillness
There comes a battle-cry—
The song that led those marching feet
To conquer, or to die.

"Yes, rally round the flag, boys!"
With tears she hears the song,
And her thoughts go back to the boys in blue,
That army, brave and strong—
Then Peace creeps in amid the pain.

The dead are as dear as the living,
And back of the song is the silence,
And back of the silence—Thanksgiving.

In the Flash of a Jewel

Certain barbaric instincts in the human race seem to be ineradicable. It is but a step from the painted savage, gorgeous in his beads and wampum, to my lady of fashion, who wears a tiara upon her stately head, chains and collars of precious stones at her throat, bracelets on her white arms, and innumerable rings upon her dainty fingers. Wise men may decry the baleful fascination of jewels, but, none the less, the jeweller's window continues to draw the crowd.

Like brilliant moths that appear only at night, jewels are tabooed in the day hours. Dame Fashion sternly condemns gems in the day time as evidence of hopelessly bad taste. No jewels are permitted in any ostentatious way, and yet a woman may, even in good society, wear a few thousand dollars' worth of precious stones, without seeming to be overdressed, provided the occasion is appropriate, as in the case of functions held in darkened rooms.

In the evening when shoulders are bared and light feet tread fantastic measures in a ball room, which is literally a bower of roses, there seems to be no limit as regards jewels. In such an assembly a woman may, without appearing overdressed, adorn herself with diamonds amounting to a small fortune.

During a season of grand opera in Chicago, a beautiful white-haired woman sat in the same box night after night without attracting particular attention, except as a woman of acknowledged beauty. At a glance it might be thought that her dress, although elegant, was rather simple, but an enterprising reporter discovered that her gown of rare old lace, with the pattern picked out here and there with chip diamonds, had cost over fifty-five thousand dollars. The tiara, collar, and few rings she wore, swelled the grand total to more than three hundred thousand dollars.

Diamonds, rubies, sapphires, emeralds, pearls, and opals—these precious stones have played a tremendous part in the world's history. Empires have been bartered for jewels, and for a string of pearls many a woman has sold her soul. It is said that pearls mean tears, yet they are favourite gifts for brides, and no maiden fears to wear them on her way up the aisle where her bridegroom waits.

A French writer claims that if it be true that the oyster can be forced to make as many pearls as may be required of it, the jewel will become so common that my lady will no longer care to decorate herself with its pale splendour. Whether or not this will ever be the case, it is certain that few gems have played a more conspicuous part in history than this.

Not only have we Cleopatra's reckless draught, but there is also a story of a noble Roman who dissolved in vinegar and drank a pearl worth a million sesterces, which had adorned the ear of the woman he loved. But the cold-hearted chemist declares that an acid which could dissolve a pearl would also dissolve the person who swallowed it, so those two legends must vanish with many others that have shrivelled up under the searching gaze of science.

There is another interesting story about the destruction of a pearl. During the reign of Elizabeth, a haughty Spanish ambassador was boasting at the Court of England of the great riches of his king. Sir Thomas Gresham, wishing to get even with the bragging Castilian, replied that some of Elizabeth's subjects would spend as much at one meal as Philip's whole kingdom could produce in a day! To prove this statement, Sir Thomas invited the Spaniard to dine with him, and having ground up a costly Eastern pearl the Englishman coolly swallowed it.

Going back to the dimness of early times, we find that many of the ancients preferred green gems to all other stones. The emerald was thought to have many virtues. It kept evil spirits at a distance, it restored failing sight, it could unearth mysteries, and when it turned yellow its owner knew to a certainty that the woman he loved was false to him.

The ruby flashes through all Oriental romances. This stone banished sadness and sin. A serpent with a ruby in its mouth was considered an appropriate betrothal ring.

The most interesting ruby of history is set in the royal diadem of England. It is called the Black Prince's ruby. In the days when the Moors ruled Granada, when both the men and the women of that race sparkled with gems, and even the ivory covers of their books were sometimes set with precious stones, the Spanish king, Don Pedro the Cruel, obtained this stone from a Moorish prince whom he had caused to be murdered.

It was given by Don Pedro to the Black Prince, and half a century later it glowed on the helmet of that most picturesque of England's kings, Henry V, at the battle of Agincourt.

The Scotchman, Sir James Melville, saw this jewel during his famous visit to the Court of Elizabeth, when the Queen showed him some of the treasures in her cabinet, the most valued of these being the portrait of Leicester.

"She showed me a fair ruby like a great racket ball," he says. "I desired she would send to my queen either this or the Earl of Leicester's picture." But Elizabeth cherished both the ruby and the portrait, so she sent Marie Stuart a diamond instead.

Poets have lavished their fancies upon the origin of the opal, but no one seems to know why it is considered unlucky. Women who laugh at superstitions of all kinds are afraid to wear an opal, and a certain jeweller at the head of one of the largest establishments in a great city has carried his fear to such a length that he will not keep one in his establishment—not only this, but it is said that he has even been known to throw an opal ring out of the window. The offending stone had been presented to his daughter, but this fact was not allowed to weigh against his superstition. It is understood when he entertains that none of his guests will wear opals, and this wish is faithfully respected.

The story goes that the opal was discovered at the same time that kissing was invented. A young shepherd on the hills of Greece found a pretty pebble one day, and wishing to give it to a beautiful shepherdess who stood near him, he let her take it from his lips with hers, as the hands of neither of them were clean.

Many a battle royal has been waged for the possession of a diamond, and several famous diamonds are known by name throughout the world. Among these are the Orloff, the Koh-i-noor, the Regent, the Real Paragon, and the Sanci, besides the enormous stone which was sent to King Edward from South Africa. This has been cut but not yet named.

The Orloff is perhaps the most brilliant of all the famous group. Tradition says that it was once one of the eyes of an Indian idol and was supposed to have been the origin of all light. A French grenadier of Pondicherry deserted his regiment, adopted the religion and manners of the Brahmans, worshipped at the shrine of the idol whose eyes were light itself, stole the brightest one, and escaped.

A sea captain bought it from him for ten thousand dollars and sold it to a Jew for sixty thousand dollars. An Armenian named Shafras bought it from the Jew, and after a time Count Orloff paid $382,500 for this and a title of Russian nobility.

He presented the wonderful refractor of light to the Empress Catherine who complimented Orloff by naming it after him. This magnificent stone, which weighs one hundred and ninety-five carats, now forms the apex of the Russian crown.

The Real Paragon was in 1861 the property of the Rajah of Mattan. It was then uncut and weighed three hundred and seven carats. The Governor of Batavia was very anxious to bring it to Europe. He offered the Rajah one hundred and fifty thousand dollars and two warships with their guns and ammunition, but the offer was contemptuously refused. Very little is known of its history. It is now owned by the Government of Portugal and is pledged as security for a very large sum of money.

It has been said that one could carry the Koh-i-noor in one end of a silk purse and balance it in the other end with a gold eagle and a gold dollar, and never feel the difference in weight, while the value of the gem in gold could not be transported in less than four dray loads!

Tradition says that Karna, King of Anga, owned it three thousand years ago. The King of Lahore, one of the Indies, heard that the King of Cabul, one of the lesser princes, had in his possession the largest and purest diamond in the world. Lahore invited Cabul to visit him, and when he had him in his power, demanded the treasure. Cabul, however, had suspected treachery, and brought an imitation of the Koh-i-noor. He of course expostulated, but finally surrendered the supposed diamond.

The lapidary who was employed to mount it pronounced it a piece of crystal, whereupon the royal old thief sent soldiers who ransacked the palace of the King of Cabul from top to bottom, in vain. At last, however, after a long search, a servant betrayed his master, and the gem was found in a pile of ashes.

After the annexation of the Punjab in 1849, the Koh-i-noor was given up to the British, and at a meeting of the Punjab Board was handed to John (afterward Lord) Lawrence who placed it in his waistcoat pocket and forgot the treasure. While at a public meeting some time later, he suddenly remembered it, hurried home and asked his servant if he had seen a small box which he had left in his waistcoat pocket.

"Yes, sahib," the man replied; "I found it, and put in your drawer."

"Bring it here," said Lawrence, and the servant produced it.

"Now," said his master, "open it and see what it contains."

The old native obeyed, and after removing the folds of linen, he said: "There is nothing here but a piece of glass."

"Good," said Lawrence, with a sigh of relief, "you can leave it with me."

The Sanci diamond belonged to Charles the Bold, Duke of Burgundy, who wore it in his hat at the battle of Nancy, where he fell. A Swiss soldier found it and sold it for a gulden to a clergyman of Baltimore. It passed into the possession of Anton, King of Portugal, who was obliged to sell it, the price being a million francs.

It shortly afterward became the property of a Frenchman named Sanci, whose descendant being sent as an ambassador, was required by the King to give the diamond as a pledge. The servant carrying it to the King was attacked by robbers on the way and murdered, not, however, until he had swallowed the diamond. His master, feeling sure of his faithfulness, caused the body to be opened and found the gem in his stomach. This gem came into the possession of the Crown of England, and James II carried it with him to France in 1688.

From James it passed to his friend and patron, Louis XIV, and to his descendants, until the Duchess of Berry at the Restoration sold it to the Demidoffs for six hundred and twenty-five thousand francs.

It was worth a million and a half of francs when Prince Paul Demidoff wore it in his hat at a great fancy ball given in honour of Count Walewski, the Minister of Napoleon III—and lost it during the ball! Everybody was wild with excitement when the loss was announced—everybody but Prince Paul Demidoff. After an hour's search the Sanci was found under a chair.

After more than two centuries, "the Regent is," as Saint-Simon described it in 1717, "a brilliant, inestimable and unique." Its density is rather higher than that of the usual diamond, and it weighs upwards of one hundred and thirty carats. This stone was found in India by a slave, who, to conceal it, made a wound in his leg and wrapped the gem in the bandages. Reaching the coast, he intrusted himself and his secret to an English captain, who took the gem, threw the slave overboard, and sold his ill-gotten gains to a native merchant for five thousand dollars.

It afterwards passed into the hands of Pitt, Governor of St. George, who sold it in 1717 to the Duke of Orleans, then Regent of France, for $675,000. Before the end of the eighteenth century the stone had more than trebled in worth, and we can only wonder what it ought to bring now with its "perfect whiteness, its regular form, and its absolute freedom from stain or flaw!"

The collection belonging to the Sultan of Turkey, which is probably the finest in the world, dates prior to the discovery of America, and undoubtedly came from Asia. One Turkish pasha alone left to the Empire at his death, seven table-cloths embroidered with diamonds, and bushels of fine pearls.

In the war with Russia, in 1778, Turkey borrowed $30,000,000 from the Ottoman Bank on the security of the crown jewels. The cashier of the bank was admitted to the treasure-chamber and was told to help himself until he had enough to secure his advances.

"I selected enough," he says, "to secure the bank against loss in any event, but the removal of the gems I took made no appreciable gap in the accumulation."

In the imperial treasury of the Sultan, the first room is the richest in notable objects. The most conspicuous of these is a great throne or divan of beaten gold, occupying the entire centre of the room, and set with precious stones: pearls, rubies, and emeralds, thousands of them, covering the entire surface in a geometrical mosaic pattern. This specimen of barbaric magnificence was part of the spoils of war taken from one of the shahs of Persia.

Much more interesting and beautiful, however, is another canopied throne or divan, placed in the upper story of the same building. This is a genuine work of old Turkish art which dates from some time during the second half of the sixteenth century. It is a raised square seat, on which the Sultan sat cross-legged. At each angle there rises a square vertical shaft supporting a canopy, with a minaret or pinnacle surmounted by a rich gold and jewelled finial. The entire height of the throne is nine or ten feet. The materials are precious woods, ebony, sandal-wood, etc., with shell, mother-of-pearl, silver, and gold.

The entire piece is decorated inside and out with a branching floriated design in mother-of-pearl marquetry, in the style of the fine early Persian painted tiles, and the centre of each of the principal leaves and flowers is set with splendid *cabochon* gems, fine balass rubies, emeralds, sapphires, and pearls.

Pendant from the roof of the canopy, and in a position which would be directly over the head of the Sultan, is a golden cord, on which is hung a large heart-shaped ornament of gold, chased and perforated with floriated work, and beneath it hangs a huge uncut emerald of fine colour, but of triangular shape, four inches in diameter, and an inch and a half thick.

Richly decorated arms and armour form a conspicuous feature of the contents of all three of these rooms. The most notable work in this class in the first apartment is a splendid suit of mixed chain and plate mail, wonderfully damascened and jewelled, worn by Sultan Murad IV, in 1638, at the taking of Bagdad.

Near to it is a scimetar, probably a part of the panoply of the same monarch. Both the hilt and the greater part of the broad scabbard of this weapon are incrusted with large table diamonds, forming checkerwork, all the square stones being regularly and symmetrically cut, of exactly the same size— upward of half an inch across. There are many other sumptuous works of art which are similarly adorned.

Rightfully first among the world's splendid coronets stands the State Crown of England. It was made in 1838 with jewels taken from old crowns and others furnished by command of the Queen.

It consists of diamonds, pearls, rubies, sapphires, and emeralds, set in silver and gold. It has a crimson velvet cap with ermine border; it is lined with white silk and weighs about forty ounces. The lower part of the band above the ermine border consists of a row of one hundred and ninety-nine pearls, and the upper part of this band has one hundred and twelve pearls, between which, in the front of the crown, is a large sapphire which was purchased for it by George IV.

At the back is a sapphire of smaller size and six others, three on each side, between which are eight emeralds. Above and below the sapphires are fourteen diamonds, and around the eight emeralds are one hundred and twenty-eight diamonds. Between the emeralds and sapphires are sixteen ornaments, containing one hundred and sixty diamonds. Above the band are eight sapphires, surmounted by eight diamonds, between which are eight festoons, consisting of one hundred and forty-eight diamonds.

In the front of the crown and in the centre of a diamond Maltese cross is the famous ruby of the Black Prince. Around this ruby to form the cross are seventy-five brilliant diamonds. Three other Maltese crosses, forming the two sides and back of the crown, have emerald centres, and each contains between one and two hundred brilliant diamonds. Between the four Maltese crosses are four ornaments in the form of the French *fleur-de-lis*, with four rubies in the centre, and surrounded by rose diamonds.

From the Maltese crosses issue four imperial arches, composed of oak leaves and acorns embellished with hundreds of magnificent jewels. From the upper part of the arches are suspended four large pendant pear-shaped pearls, with rose diamond caps. Above the arch stands the mound, thickly set with brilliants. The cross on the summit has a rose cut sapphire in the centre, surrounded by diamonds.

A gem is said to represent "condensed wealth," and it is also condensed history. The blood of a ruby, the faint moonlight lustre of a pearl, the green glow of an emerald, and the dazzling white light of a diamond—in what unfailing magic lies their charm? Tiny bits of crystal as they appear to be— even the Orloff diamond could be concealed in a child's hand—yet kings and queens have played for stakes like these. Battle and murder have been done for them, honour bartered and kingdoms lost, but the old magic beauty never fades, and to-day, as always, sin and beauty, side, by side, are mirrored in the flash of a jewel.

The Coming of My Ship

Straight to the sunrise my ship's sails are leaning,
Brave at the masthead her new colours fly;
Down on the shore, her lips trembling with meaning,
Love waits, but unanswering, I heed not her cry.
The gold of the East shall be mine in full measure,
My ship shall come home overflowing with treasure,
And love is not need, but only a pleasure,
So I wait for my ship to come in.

Silent, half troubled, I wait in the shadow,
No sail do I see between me and the dawn;
Out in the blue and measureless meadow,
My ship wanders widely, but Love has not gone.
"My arms await thee," she cries in her pleading,
"Why wait for its coming, when I am thy needing?"
I pass by in stillness, all else unheeding,
And wait for my ship to come in.

See, in the East, surrounded by splendour,
My sail glimmers whitely in crimson and blue;
I turn back to Love, my heart growing tender,
"Now I have gold and leisure for you.
Jewels she brings for thy white breast's adorning,
Measures of gold beyond a queen's scorning"—
To-night I shall rest—joy comes in the morning,
So I wait for my ship to come in.

Remembering waters beat cold on the shore,
And the grey sea in sadness grows old;
I listen in vain for Love's pleading once more,
While my ship comes with spices and gold.
The sea birds cry hoarsely, for this is their songing,
On masthead and colours their white wings are thronging,
But my soul throbs deep with love and with longing,
And I wait for my ship to come in.

Romance and the Postman

A letter! Do the charm and uncertainty of it ever fade? Who knows what may be written upon the pages within!

Far back, in a dim, dream-haunted childhood, the first letter came to me. It was "a really, truly letter," properly stamped and addressed, and duly delivered by the postman. With what wonder the chubby fingers broke the seal! It did not matter that there was an inclosure to one's mother, and that the thing itself was written by an adoring relative; it was a personal letter, of private and particular importance, and that day the postman assumed his rightful place in one's affairs.

In the treasure box of many a grandmother is hidden a pathetic scrawl that the baby made for her and called "a letter." To the alien eye, it is a mere tangle of pencil marks, and the baby himself, grown to manhood, with children of his own, would laugh at the yellowed message, which is put away with his christening robe and his first shoes, but to one, at least, it speaks with a deathless voice.

It is written in books and papers that some unhappy mortals are swamped with mail. As a lady recently wrote to the President of the United States: "I suppose you get so many letters that when you see the postman coming down the street, you don't care whether he has anything for you or not."

Indeed, the President might well think the universe had gone suddenly wrong if the postman passed him by, but there are compensations in everything. The First Gentleman of the Republic must inevitably miss the pleasant emotions which letters bring to the most of us.

The clerks and carriers in the business centres may be pardoned if they lose sight of the potentialities of the letters that pass through their hands. When a skyscraper is a postal district in itself, there is no time for the man in grey to think of the burden he carries, save as so many pounds of dead weight, becoming appreciably lighter at each stop. But outside the hum and bustle, on quiet streets and secluded by-ways, there are faces at the windows, watching eagerly for the mail.

The progress of the postman is akin to a Roman triumph, for in his leathern pack lies Fate. Long experience has given him a sixth sense, as if the letters breathed a hint of their contents through their superscriptions.

The business letter, crisp and to the point, has an atmosphere of its own, even where cross lines of typewriting do not show through the envelope.

The long, rambling, friendly hand is distinctive, and if it has been carried in the pocket a long time before mailing, the postman knows that the writer is a married woman with a foolish trust in her husband.

Circulars addressed mechanically, at so much a thousand, never deceive the postman, though the recipient often opens them with pleasurable sensations, which immediately sink to zero. And the love-letters! The carrier is a veritable Sherlock Holmes when it comes to them.

Gradually he becomes acquainted with the inmost secrets of those upon his route. Friendship, love, and marriage, absence and return, death, and one's financial condition, are all as an open book to the man in grey. Invitations, cards, wedding announcements, forlorn little letters from those to whom writing is not as easy as speech, childish epistles with scrap pictures pasted on the outside, all give an inkling of their contents to the man who delivers them.

When the same bill comes to the same house for a long and regular period, then ceases, even the carrier must feel relieved to know that it has been paid. When he isn't too busy, he takes a friendly look at the postal cards, and sometimes saves a tenant in a third flat the weariness of two flights of stairs by shouting the news up the tube!

If the dweller in a tenement has ingratiating manners, he may learn how many papers, and letters are being stuffed into the letter-box, by a polite inquiry down the tube when the bell rings. Through the subtle freemasonry of the postman's voice a girl knows that her lover has not forgotten her—and her credit is good for the "two cents due" if the tender missive is overweight.

"All the world loves a lover," and even the busy postman takes a fatherly interest in the havoc wrought by Cupid along his route. The little blind god knows neither times nor seasons—all alike are his own—but the man in grey, old and spectacled though he may be, is his confidential messenger.

Love-letters are seemingly immortal. A clay tablet on which one of the Pharaohs wrote, asking for the heart and hand of a beautiful foreign princess, is now in the British Museum. But suppose the postman had not been sure-footed, and all the clay letters had been smashed into fragments in a single grand catastrophe! What a stir in high places, what havoc in Church and State, and how many fond hearts broken, if the postman had fallen down!

"Nothing feeds the flame like a letter," said Emerson; "it has intent, personality, secrecy." Flimsy and frail as it is, so easily torn or destroyed, the love-letter many times outlasts the love. Even the Father of his Country, though he has been dead this hundred years or more, has left behind him a love-letter, ragged and faded, but still legible, beginning: "My Dearest Life and Love."

"Matter is indestructible," so the scientists say, but what of the love-letter that is reduced to ashes? Does its passion live again in some far-off violet flame, or, rising from its dust, bloom once more in a fragrant rose, to touch the lips of another love?

In countless secret places, the tender missives are hidden, for the lover must always keep his joy in tangible form, to be sure that it was not a dream. They fly through the world by day and night, like white-winged birds that can say, "I love you"—over mountain, hill, stream, and plain; past sea and lake and river, through the desert's fiery heat and amid the throbbing pulses of civilisation, with never a mistake, to bring exquisite rapture to another heart and wings of light to the loved one's soul.

Under the pillow of the maiden, her lover's letter brings visions of happiness too great for the human heart to hold. Even in her dreams, her fingers tighten upon his letter—the visible assurance of his unchanging and unchangeable love.

When the bugle sounds the charge, and dimly through the flash and flame the flag signals "Follow!" many a heart, leaping to answer with the hot blood of youth, finds a sudden tenderness in the midst of its high courage, from the loving letter which lies close to the soldier's breast.

Bunker Hill and Gettysburg, Moscow and the Wilderness, Waterloo, Mafeking, and San Juan—the old blood-stained fields and the modern scenes of terror have all alike known the same message and the same thrill. The faith and hope of the living, the kiss and prayer of the dying, the cries of the wounded, and the hot tears of those who have parted forever, are on the blood-stained pages of the love-letters that have gone to war.

"*Ich liebe Dich*," "*Je t'aime*," or, in our dear English speech, "I love you,"—it is all the same, for the heart knows the universal language, the words of which are gold, bedewed with tears that shine like precious stones.

Every attic counts old love-letters among its treasures, and when the rain beats on the roof and grey swirls of water are blown against the pane, one may sit among the old trunks and boxes and bring to light the loves of days gone by.

The little hair-cloth trunk, with its rusty lock and broken hinges, brings to mind a rosy-cheeked girl in a poke bonnet, who went a-visiting in the stage-coach. Inside is the bonnet itself—white, with a gorgeous trimming of pink "lute-string" ribbon, which has faded into ashes of roses at the touch of the kindly years.

From the trunk comes a musty fragrance—lavender, sweet clover, rosemary, thyme, and the dried petals of roses that have long since crumbled to dust. Scraps of brocade and taffeta, yellowed lingerie, and a quaint old wedding gown, daguerreotypes in ornate cases, and then the letters, tied with faded ribbon, in a package by themselves.

The fingers unconsciously soften to their task, for the letters are old and yellow, and the ink has faded to brown. Every one was cut open with the scissors, not hastily torn according to our modern fashion, but in a slow and seemly manner, as befits a solemn occasion.

Perhaps the sweet face of a great-grandmother grew much perplexed at the sight of a letter in an unfamiliar hand, and perhaps, too, as is the way of womankind, she studied the outside a long time before she opened it. As the months passed by, the handwriting became familiar, but a coquettish grandmother may have flirted a bit with the letter, and put it aside—until she could be alone.

All the important letters are in the package, from the first formal note asking permission to call, which a womanly instinct bade the maiden put aside, to the last letter, written when twilight lay upon the long road they had travelled together, but still beginning: "My Dear and Honoured Wife."

Bits of rosemary and geranium, lemon verbena, tuberose, and heliotrope, fragile and whitened, but still sweet, fall from the opened letters and rustle softly as they fall.

Far away in the "peace which passeth all understanding," the writer of the letters sleeps, but the old love keeps a fragrance that outlives the heart in which it bloomed.

At night, when the fires below are lighted, and childish voices make the old house ring with laughter, Memory steals into the attic to sing softly of the past, as a mother croons her child to sleep.

Rocking in a quaint old attic chair, with the dear familiar things of home gathered all about her, Memory's voice is sweet, like a harp tuned in the minor mode when the south wind sweeps the strings.

Bunches of herbs swing from the rafters and fill the room with the wholesome scent of an old-fashioned garden, where rue and heartsease grew. With the fragrance comes the breath from that garden of Mnemosyne, where the simples for heartache nod beside the River of Forgetfulness.

In a flash the world is forgotten, and into the attic come dear faces from that distant land of childhood, where a strange enchantment glorified the commonplace, and made the dreams of night seem real. Footsteps that have long been silent are heard upon the attic floor, and voices, hushed for years, whisper from the shadows from the other end of the room.

A moonbeam creeps into the attic and transfigures the haunted chamber with a sheen of silver mist. From the spinning-wheel come a soft hum and a delicate whir; then a long-lost voice breathes the first notes of an old, old song. The melody changes to a minuet, and the lady in the portrait moves, smiling, from the tarnished gilt frame that surrounds her—then a childish voice says: "Mother, are you asleep?"

Down the street the postman passes, bearing his burden of joy and pain: letters from far-off islands, where the Stars and Stripes gleam against a forest of palms; from the snow-bound fastnesses of the North, where men are searching for gold; from rose-scented valleys and violet fields, where the sun forever shines, and from lands across the sea, where men speak an alien tongue—single messages from one to another; letters that plead for pardon cross the paths of those that are meant to stab; letters written in jest too often find grim earnest at the end of their journey, and letters written in all tenderness meet misunderstandings and pain, when the postman brings them home; letters that deal with affairs of state and shape the destiny of a nation; tidings of happiness and sorrow, birth and death, love and trust, and the thousand pangs of trust betrayed; an hundred joys and as many griefs are all in the postman's hands.

No wonder, then, that there is a stir in the house, that eyes brighten, hearts beat quickly, and eager steps hasten to the door of destiny, when the postman rings the bell!

A Summer Reverie

I sit on the shore of the deep blue sea
As the tide comes rolling in,
And wonder, as roaming in sunlit dreams,
The cause of the breakers' din.

For each of the foam-crowned billows
Has a wonderful story to tell,
And the surge's mystical music
Seems wrought by a fairy spell.

I wander through memory's portals,
Through mansions dim and vast,
And gaze at the beautiful pictures
That hang in the halls of the past.

And dream-faces gather around me,
With voices soft and low,
To draw me back to the pleasures
Of the lands of long ago.

There are visions of beauty and splendour,
And a fame that I never can win—
Far out on the deep they are sailing—
My ships that will never come in.

A Vignette

It was a muddy down-town corner and several people stood in the cold, waiting for a street-car. A stand of daily papers was on the sidewalk, guarded by two little newsboys. One was much younger than the other, and he rolled two marbles back and forth in the mud by the curb. Suddenly his attention was attracted by something bright above him, and he looked up into a bunch of red carnations a young lady held in her hands. He watched them eagerly, seemingly unable to take his eyes from the feast of colour. She saw the hungry look in the little face, and put one into his hand. He was silent, until his brother said: "Say thanky to the lady." He whispered his thanks, and then she bent down and pinned the blossom upon his ragged jacket, while the big policeman on the corner smiled approvingly.

"My, but you're gay now, and you can sell all your papers," the bigger boy said tenderly.

"Yep, I can sell 'em now, sure!"

Out of the crowd on the opposite corner came a tiny, dark-skinned Italian girl, with an accordion slung over her shoulder by a dirty ribbon; she made straight for the carnations and fearlessly cried, "Lady, please give me a flower!" She got one, and quickly vanished in the crowd.

The young woman walked up the street to a flower-stand to replenish her bunch of carnations, and when she returned, another dark-skinned mite rushed up to her without a word, only holding up grimy hands with a gesture of pathetic appeal. Another brilliant blossom went to her, and the young woman turned to follow her; on through the crowd the child fled, until she reached the corner where her mother stood, seamed and wrinkled and old, with the dark pathetic eyes of sunny Italy. She held the flower out to her, and the weary mother turned and snatched it eagerly, then pressed it to her lips, and kissed it as passionately as if it had been the child who brought it to her.

Just then the car came, and the big grey policeman helped the owner of the carnations across the street, and said as he put her on the car, "Lady, you've sure done them children a good turn to-day."

Meditation

I sail through the realms of the long ago,
Wafted by fancy and visions frail,
On the river Time with its gentle flow,
In a silver boat with a golden sail.

My dreams, in the silence are hurrying by
On the brooklet of Thought where I let them flow,
And the "lilies nod to the sound of the stream"
As I sail through the realms of the long ago.

On the shores of life's deep-flowing stream
Are my countless sorrows and heartaches, too,
And the hills of hope are but dimly seen,
Far in the distance, near heaven's blue.

I find that my childish thoughts and dreams
Lie strewn on the sands by the cruel blast
That scattered my hopes on the restless streams
That flow through the mystic realms of the past.

Pointers for the Lords of Creation

Some wit has said that the worst vice in the world is advice, and it is also quite true that one ignorant, though well-meaning person can sometimes accomplish more damage in a short time, than a dozen people who start out for the purpose of doing mischief.

The newspapers and periodicals of to-day are crowded with advice to women, and while much of it is found in magazines for women, written and edited by men, it is also true that a goodly quantity of it comes from feminine writers; it is all along the same lines, however, the burden of effort being to teach the weaker sex how to become more attractive and more lovable to the lords of creation. It is, of course, all intended for our good, for if we can only please the men, and obey their slightest wish even before they take the trouble to mention the matter, we can then be perfectly happy.

A man can sit down any day and give us directions enough to keep us busy for a lifetime, and we seldom or never return the compliment. This is manifestly unfair, and so this little preachment is meant for the neglected and deserving men, and for them only, so that all women who have read thus far are invited to leave the matter right here and turn their attention to the column of "Advice to Women" which they can find in almost any periodical.

In the first place, gentlemen, we must admit that you do keep us guessing, though we do not sit up nights nor lose much sleep over your queer notions.

We can't ask you many questions, either, dear brethren, for, as you know, you rather like to fib to us, and sometimes we are able to find it out, and then we never believe you any more.

We may venture, however, to ask small favours of you, and one of these is that you do not wear red ties. You look so nice in quiet colours that we dislike exceedingly to have you make crazy quilts of yourselves, and that is just what you do when you begin experimenting with colours which we naturally associate with the "cullud pussons."

And a cane may be very ornamental, but it's of no earthly use, and we would rather you would not carry it when you go out with us.

Never tell us you haven't had time to come and see us, or write to us, because we know perfectly well that if you wanted to badly enough, you would take the time, so the excuse makes us even madder than does the neglect. Still, when you don't want to come, we would not have you do it for anything.

There is an old saying that "absence makes the heart grow fonder"—so it does—of the other fellow. We don't propose to shed any tears over you; we simply go to the theatre with the other man and have an extremely good time.

When you are very, very bright, you can manage some way not to allow us to forget you for a minute, nor give us much time to think of anything else.

When we are angry, for heaven's sake don't ask us why, because that shows your lack of penetration. Just simply call yourself a brute, and say you are utterly unworthy of even our faint regard, and you will soon realise that this covers a lot of ground, and everything will be all right in a few minutes.

And whatever you do, don't show any temper yourself. A woman requires of a man that he shall be as immovable as the rock of Gibraltar, no matter what she does to him. And you play your strongest card when you don't mind our tantrums—even though it's a state secret we are telling you.

Don't get huffy when you meet us with another man; in nine cases out of ten, that's just what we do it for. And don't make the mistake of retaliating by asking another girl somewhere. You'll have a perfectly miserable time if you do, both then and afterward.

When you do come to see us, it is not at all nice to spend the entire evening talking about some other girl. How would you like to have the graces of some other man continually dinned into your ears? Sometimes we take that way in order to get a rest from your overweening raptures over the absent girl.

We have a well-defined suspicion that you talk us over with your chums and compare notes. But, bless you, it can't possibly hold a candle to the thorough and impartial discussions that some of you get when girls are together, either in small bevies, or with only one chosen friend. And we don't very much care what you say about us, for a man never judges a woman by the opinion of any one else, but another woman's opinion counts for a great deal with us, so you would better be careful.

If you are going to say things that you don't mean, try to stamp them with the air of sincerity—if you can once get a woman to fully believe in your sincerity, you have gone a long way toward her heart.

Haven't you found out that women are not particularly interested in anecdotes? Please don't tell us more than fifteen in the same evening.

And don't begin to make love to us before you have had time to make a favourable impression along several lines—a man, as well as a woman, loses ground and forfeits respect by making himself too cheap.

If a girl runs and screams when she has been caught standing under the mistletoe, it means that she will not object; if she stiffens up and glares at you, it means that she does. The same idea is sometimes delicately conveyed by the point of a pin. But a woman will be able to forgive almost anything which you can make her believe was prompted by her own attractiveness, at least unless she knows men fairly well.

You know, of course, that we will not show your letters, nor tell when you ask us to marry you and are refused. This much a woman owes to any man who has honoured her with an offer of marriage—to keep his perfect trust sacredly in her own heart. Even her future husband has no business to know of this—it is her lover's secret, and she has no right to betray it.

Keeping the love-letters and the offers of marriage from any honourable man safe from a prying world are points of honour which all good women possess, although we may sometimes quote certain things from your letters, as you do from ours.

There's nothing you can tell a woman which will please her quite so much as that knowing her has made you better, especially if you can prove it by showing a decided upward tendency in your morals. That's your good right bower, but don't play it too often—keep it for special occasions.

There's one mistake you make, dear brethren, and that is telling a woman you love her as soon as you find it out yourself, and the most of you will do that very thing. There is one case on record where a man waited fifteen minutes, but he nearly died of the strain. The trouble is that you seldom stop to consider whether we are ready to hear you or not, nor whether the coast is clear, nor what the chances are in your favour. You simply relieve your mind, and trust in your own wonderful charms to accomplish the rest.

And we wish that when the proper time comes for you to speak your mind you'd try to do it artistically. Of course you can't write it, unless you are far away from her, for if you can manage an opportunity to speak, a resort to the pen is cowardly. And don't mind our evading the subject—we always do that on principle, but please don't be scared, or at least don't show it, whatever you may feel. If there is one thing a woman dislikes more than another it is a man who shows cowardice at the crucial point in life.

Every man, except yourself, dear reader, is conceited. And one particular sort of it makes us very, very weary. You are so blinded by your own perfections, so sure that we are desperately in love with you, that you sometimes give us little unspoken suggestions to that effect, and then our disgust is beyond words.

Another cowardly thing you sometimes do, and that is to say that we have spoiled your life—that we could have made you anything we pleased—and that you are going straight to perdition. If one woman is all that keeps you from going to ruin, you have secured a through ticket anyway, and it's too late to save you. You don't want a woman who might marry you only out of pity, and you are not going to die of a broken heart. Men die of broken vanity, sometimes, but their hearts are pretty tough, being made of healthy muscle.

You get married very much as you go down town in the morning. You run, like all possessed, until you catch your car, and then you sit down and read your newspaper. When you think your wife looks unusually well, it would not hurt you in the least to tell her so, and the way you leave her in the morning is going to settle her happiness for the day, though she may be too proud to let you know that it makes any difference. Women are quick to detect a sham, and they don't want you to say anything that you don't feel, but you are pretty sure to feel tenderly toward her sometimes, careless though you may be, and then is the time to tell her so. You don't want to wait until she is dead, and then buy a lily to put on her coffin. You'd better bring her the lily some time when you've been cross and grumpy.

But don't imagine that a present of any kind ever atones for a hurt that has been given in words. There's nothing you can say which is more manly or which will do you both so much good as the simple "forgive me" when you have been wrong.

Rest assured, gentlemen, that you who spend the most of your evenings in other company, and too often find fault with your meals when you come home, are the cause of many sorrowful talks among the women who are wise enough to know, even though your loyal wife may put up a brave front in your defense.

How often do you suppose the brave woman who loves you has been actually driven in her agony to some married friend whom she can trust and upon her sympathetic bosom has cried until she could weep no more, simply because of your thoughtless neglect? How often do you think she has planned little things to make your home-coming pleasant, which you have never noticed? And how often do you suppose she has desperately fought down the heartache and tried to believe that your absorption in business is the reason for your forgetfulness of her?

Do you ever think of these things? Do you ever think of the days before you were sure of her, when you treasured every line of her letters, and would have bartered your very hopes of heaven for the earthly life with her?

But perhaps you can hardly be expected to remember the wild sprint that you made from the breakfast table to the street-car.

Transition

I am thy Pleasure. See, my face is fair—
With silken strands of joy I twine thee round;
Life has enough of stress—forget with me!
Wilt thou not stay? Then go, thou art not bound.

I am thy Pastime. Let me be to thee
A daily refuge from the haunting fears
That bind thee, choke thee, fill thy soul with woe.
Seek thou my hand, let me assuage thy tears.

I am thy Habit. Nay, start not, thy will
Is yet supreme, for art thou not a man?
Then draw me close to thee, for life is brief—
A little space to pass as best one can.

I am thy Passion. Thou shalt cling to me
Through all the years to come. The silken cord
Of Pleasure has become a stronger bond,
Not to be cleft, nor loosened at a word.

I am thy Master. Thou shalt crush for me
The grapes of truth for wine of sacrifice;
My clanking chains were forged for such as thee,
I am thy Master—yea, I am thy vice!

The Superiority of Man

Without pausing to inquire why savages and barbarians are capable of producing college professors, who sneer at the source from which they sprung, we may accept for the moment the masculine hypothesis of intellectual superiority. Some women have been heard to say that they wish they had been born men, but there is no man bold enough to say that he would like to be a woman.

If woman can produce a reasoning being, it follows that she herself must be capable of reasoning, since a stream can rise no higher than its fountain. And yet the bitter truth stares us in the face. We have no Shakespeare, Michelangelo, or Beethoven; our Darwins, our Schumanns are mute and inglorious; our Miltons, Raphaels, and Herbert Spencers have not arrived.

Call the roll of the great and how many women's names will be found there? Scarcely enough to enable you to call the company mixed.

No woman in her senses wishes to be merely the female of man. She aspires to be distinctly different—to exercise her varied powers in wholly different ways. Ex-President Roosevelt said: "Equality does not imply identity of function." We do not care to put in telephones or to collect fares on a street-car.

Primitive man set forth from his cave to kill an animal or two, then repaired to a secluded nook in the jungle, with other primitive men, to discuss the beginnings of politics. Primitive woman in the cave not only dressed his game, but she cooked the animal for food, made clothing of its skin, necklaces and bracelets of its teeth, passementerie of its claws, and needles of its sharper bones. What wonder that she had no time for an afternoon tea?

The man of the twentieth century has progressed immeasurably beyond this, but his wife, industrially speaking, has not gone half so far. Is she not still in some cases a cave-dweller, while he roams the highways of the world?

If a woman mends men's socks, should he not darn her lisle-thread hosiery, and run a line of machine stitching around the middle of the hem to prevent a disastrous run from a broken stitch? If she presses his ties, why should he not learn to iron her bits of fine lace?

Some one will say: "But he supports her. It is her duty."

"Yes, dear friend, but similarly does he 'support' the servant who does the same duties. He also gives her seven dollars every Monday morning, or she leaves." Are we to suppose that a wife is a woman who does general housework for board and clothes, with a few kind words thrown in?

A German lady, whom we well knew, worked all the morning attending to the comforts of her liege lord. In the dining room he was stretched out in an easy chair, while the queen of his heart brushed and repaired his clothes—yes, and blacked his boots! Doubtless for a single kiss, redolent of beer and sausages, she would have pressed his trousers. Kind words and the fragrant osculation had already saved him three dollars at his tailor's.

By such gold-brick methods, dear friends, do men get good service cheap. Would that we could do the same! Here, and gladly, we admit masculine superiority.

Our short-sightedness, our weakness for kind words, our graceful acceptance of the entire responsibility for the home, have chained us to the earth, while our lords soar. After having worked steadily for some six thousand years to populate the earth passably, some of us may now be excused from that duty.

Motherhood is a career for which especial talents are required. Very few women know how to bring up children properly. If you don't believe it, look at the difference between our angelic offspring, and the little imps next door! It is as unreasonable to suppose that all women can be good mothers as it is to suppose that all women can sing in grand opera.

And yet, let us hug to our weary hearts, in our most discouraged moments, the great soul-satisfying truth that men, no matter what they say or write, think that we are smarter than they are. Otherwise, they would not expect of us so much more than they can possibly do themselves.

In every field of woman's work outside the house, the same illustration applies. They also think that we possess greater physical strength. They chivalrously shield us from the exhausting effort of voting, but allow us to stand in the street-cars, wash dishes, push a baby carriage, and scrub the kitchen floor. Should we not be proud because they consider us so much stronger and wiser than they? Interruptions are fatal to their work, as the wife of even a business man will testify.

What would have become of Spencer's *Data of Ethics* if, while he was writing it, he had two dressmakers in the house? Should we have had *Hamlet*, if at the completion of the first act Mr. Shakespeare had given birth to twins, when he had made clothes for only one?

The great charm of marriage, as of life itself, is its unexpectedness. The only way to test a man is to marry him. If you live, it's a mushroom; if you die, it's a toadstool!

Or, as another saying goes: "Happiness after marriage is like the soap in the bath-tub; you knew it was there when you got in."

Man's clothes are ugly, but the styles change gradually. A judge on the bench may try a case lasting two weeks, and his hat will not be hopelessly behind the times when it is finished. A man can stoop to pick up a fallen magazine without pausing to remember that his front steels are not so flexible this year as they were last.

He is not distressed by the fear that some other man may have a suit just like his, or that the neighbours will think it is his last year's suit dyed.

We women fritter ourselves away upon a thousand unnecessary things. We waste our creative energies and our inspired moments upon pursuits so ephemeral that they are forgotten to-morrow. Our day's work counts for nothing when tested by the standards of eternity. We are unjust, not only to ourselves, but to the men who strive for us, for civilisation must progress very slowly when half of us are dragged by pots and pans.

A house is a material fact, but a home is a fine spiritual essence which may pervade even the humblest abode. If love means harmony, why not try a little of it in the kitchen? Better a perfect salad than a poor poem; better a fine picture than an immaculate house.

The Year of My Heart

A sigh for the spring, full flowered, promised spring,
Laid on the tender earth, and those dear days
When apple blossoms gleamed against the blue!
Ah, how the world of joyous robins sang:
"I love but you, Sweetheart, I love but you!"

A sigh for summer fled. In warm, sweet air
Her thousand singers sped on shining wing;
And all the inward life of budding grain
Throbbed with a thousand pulses, while I cling
To you, my Sweet, with passion near to pain.

A sigh for autumn past. The garnered fields
Lie desolate to-day. My heart is chill
As with a sense of dread, and on the shore
The waves beat grey and cold, and seem to say:
"No more, oh, waiting soul, oh nevermore!"

A sigh for winter come. No singing bird,
Nor harvest field, is near the path I tread;
An empty husk is all I have to keep.
The largess of my giving left me bare,
And I ask God but for His Lethe—sleep.

The Average Man

The real man is not at all on the outskirts of civilisation. He is very much in evidence and everybody knows him. He has faults and virtues, and sometimes they get so mixed up that "you cannot tell one from t'other."

He is erratic and often queer. He believes, with Emerson, that "with consistency a great soul has nothing to do." And he is, of course, "a great soul." Logical, isn't it?

The average man *thinks* that he is a born genius at love-making. Henders, in *The Professor's Love Story*, states it thus:

"Effie, ye ken there are some men ha' a power o'er women.... They're what ye might call 'dead shots.' Ye canna deny, Effie, that I'm one o' those men!"

Even though a man may be obliged to admit, in strict confidence between himself and his mirror, that he is not at all handsome, nevertheless he is certain that he has some occult influence over that strange, mystifying, and altogether unreasonable organ—a woman's heart.

The real man is conceited. Of course you are not, dear masculine reader, for you are one of the bright particular exceptions, but all of your men friends are conceited—aren't they?

And then he makes fun of his women folks because they spend so much time in front of the mirror in arranging hats and veils. But when a high wind comes up and disarranges coiffures and chapeaux alike, he takes "my ladye fair" into some obscure corner, and saying, "Pardon me, but your hat isn't quite straight," he will deftly restore that piece of millinery to its pristine position. That's nice of him, isn't it? He does very nice things quite often, this real man.

He says women are fickle. So they are, but men are fickle too, and will forget all about the absent sweetheart while contemplating the pretty girls in the street. For while "absence makes the heart grow fonder" in the case of a woman, it is presence that plays the mischief with a man, and Miss Beauty present has a very unfair advantage over Miss Sweetheart absent.

The average man thinks he is a connoisseur of feminine attractiveness. He thinks he has tact, too, but there never was a man who was blessed with much of this valuable commodity. Still, as that is a favourite delusion with so large a majority of the human race, the conceit of the ordinary masculine individual ought not to be censured too strongly.

The real man is quite an expert at flattery. Every girl he meets, if she is at all attractive, is considered the most charming lady that he ever knew. He is sure she isn't prudish enough to refuse him a kiss, and if she is, she wins not only his admiration, but that which is vastly better—his respect.

If she hates to be considered a prude and gives him the kiss, he is very sweet and appreciative at the time, but later on he confides to his chum that she is a silly sort of a girl, without a great deal of self-respect!

There are two things that the average man likes to be told. One is that his taste in dress is exceptional; the other that he is a deep student of human nature and knows the world thoroughly. This remark will make him your lifelong friend.

Again, the real man will put on more agony when he is in love than is needed for a first-class tragedy. But there's no denying that most women like that sort of thing, you, dear dainty feminine reader, being almost the only exception to this rule.

But, resuming the special line of thought, man firmly believes that woman cannot sharpen a pencil, select a necktie, throw a stone, drive a nail, or kill a mouse, and it is very certain that she cannot cook a beef-steak in the finished style of which his lordship is capable.

Yes, man has his faults as well as woman. There is a vast room for improvement on both sides, but as long as this old earth of ours turns through shadow and sunlight, through sorrow and happiness, men and women will forgive and try to forget, and will cling to, and love each other.

The Book of Love

I dreamt I saw an angel in the night,
And she held forth Love's book, limned o'er with gold,
That I might read of days of chivalry
And how men's hearts were wont to thrill of old.

Half wondering, I turned the musty leaves,
For Love's book counts out centuries as years,
And here and there a page shone out undimmed,
And here and there a page was blurred with tears.

I read of Grief, Doubt, Silence unexplained—
Of many-featured Wrong, Distrust, and Blame,
Renunciation—bitterest of all—
And yet I wandered not beyond Love's name.

At last I cried to her who held the book,
So fair and calm she stood, I see her yet;
"Why write these things within this book of Love?
Why may we not pass onward and forget?"

Her voice was tender when she answered me:
"Half child, half woman, earthy as thou art,
How should'st thou dream that Love is never Love
Unless these things beat vainly on the heart?"

The Ideal Man

He isn't nearly so scarce as one might think, but happy is the woman who finds him, for he is often a bit out of the beaten paths, sometimes in the very suburbs of our modern civilisation. He is, however, coming to the front rather slowly, to be sure, but nevertheless he is coming.

He wouldn't do for the hero of a dime novel—he isn't melancholy in his mien, nor Byronic in his morals. It is a frank, honest, manly face that looks into the other end of our observation telescope when we sweep the horizon to find something higher and better than the rank and file of humanity.

He is a gentleman, invariably courteous and refined. He is careful in his attire, but not foppish. He is chivalrous in his attitude toward woman, and as politely kind to the wrinkled old woman who scrubs his office floor as to the aristocratic belle who bows to him from her carriage.

He is scrupulously honest in all his dealings with his fellow men, and meanness of any sort is utterly beneath him. He has a happy way of seeing the humorous side of life, and he is an exceedingly pleasant companion.

When the love light shines in his eyes, kindled at the only fire where it may be lighted, he has nothing in his past of which he need be ashamed. He stands beside her and pleads earnestly and manfully for the treasure he seeks. Slowly he turns the pages of his life before her, for there is not one which can call a blush to his cheek, or to hers.

Truth, purity, honesty, chivalry, the highest manliness—all these are written therein, and she gladly accepts the clean heart which is offered for her keeping.

Her life is now another open book. To him her nature seems like a harp of a thousand strings, and every note, though it may not be strong and high, is truth itself, and most refined in tone.

So they join hands, these two: the sweetheart becomes the wife; the lover is the husband.

He is still chivalrous to every woman, but to his wife he pays the gentler deference which was the sweetheart's due. He loves her, and is not ashamed to show it. He brings her flowers and books, just as he used to do when he was teaching her to love him. He is broad-minded, and far-seeing—he believes in "a white life for two." He knows his wife has the same right to demand purity in thought, word, and deed from him, as he has to ask absolute stainlessness from her. That is why he has kept clean the pages of his life—why he keeps the record unsullied as the years go by.

He is tender in his feelings; if he goes home and finds his wife in tears, he doesn't tell her angrily to "brace up," or say, "this is a pretty welcome for a man!" He doesn't slam the door and whistle as if nothing was the matter. But he takes her in his comforting arms and speaks soothing words. If his comrades speak lightly of his devotion, he simply thinks out other blessings for the little woman who presides at his fireside.

His wife is inexpressibly dear to him, and every day he shows this, and takes pains, also, to tell her so. He admires her pretty gowns, and is glad to speak appreciatively of the becoming things she wears. He knows instinctively that it is the thoughtfulness and the little tenderness which make a woman's happiness, and he tries to make her realise that his love for her grew brighter, instead of fading, when the sweetheart blossomed into the wife. For every woman, old, wrinkled, and grey, or young and charming, likes to be loved.

The ideal man will do his utmost to make his wife realise that his devotion intensifies as the years go by.

What greater thing is there for two human souls than to feel that they are joined for life—to strengthen each other in all labour, to rest upon each other in all sorrow, to minister to each other in all pain, to be one with each other in silent unspeakable memories at the moment of the last parting?

God bless the ideal man and hasten his coming in greater numbers.

Good-Night, Sweetheart

Good-night, Sweetheart; the wingèd hours have flown;
I have forgotten all the world but thee.
Across the moon-lit deep, where stars have shone,
The surge sounds softly from the sleeping sea.

Thy heart at last hath opened to Love's key;
Remembered Aprils, glorious blooms have sown,
And now there comes the questing honey bee.
Good-night, Sweetheart; the wingèd hours have flown.

My singing soul makes music in thine own,
Thy hand upon my harp makes melody;
So close the theme and harmony have grown
I have forsaken all the world for thee.

Before thy whiteness do I bend the knee;
Thou art a queen upon a stainless throne,
Like Dian making royal jubilee,
Across the vaulted dark where stars are blown.

Within my heart thy face shines out alone,
Ah, dearest! Say for once thou lovest me!
A whisper, even, like the undertone
The surge sings slowly from the rhythmic sea.

Thy downcast eyes make answer to my plea;
A crimson mantle o'er thy cheek is thrown
Assurance more than this, there need not be,
For thus, within the silence, love is known.
Good-night, Sweetheart.

The Ideal Woman

The trend of modern thought in art and literature is toward the real, but fortunately the cherishing of the ideal has not vanished.

All of us, though we may profess to be realists, are at heart idealists, for every woman in the innermost sanctuary of her thoughts cherishes an ideal man. And every man, practical and commonplace though he be, has before him in his quiet moments a living picture of grace and beauty, which, consciously or not, is his ideal woman.

Every man instinctively admires a beautiful woman. But when he seeks a wife, he demands other qualities besides that wonderful one which is, as the proverb tells us, "only skin deep."

If men were not such strangely inconsistent beings, the world would lose half its charm. Each sex rails at the other for its inconsistency, when the real truth is that nowhere exists much of that beautiful quality which is aptly termed a "jewel."

But humanity must learn with Emerson to seek other things than consistency, and to look upon the lightning play of thought and feeling as an index of mental and moral growth.

For those who possess the happy faculty of "making the best of things," men are really the most amusing people in existence. To hear a man dilate upon the virtues and accomplishments of the ideal woman he would make his wife is a most interesting diversion, besides being a source of what may be called decorative instruction.

She must, first of all, be beautiful. No man, even in his wildest moments, ever dreamed of marrying any but a beautiful woman, yet, in nine cases out of ten when he does go to the altar, he is leading there one who is lovely only in his own eyes.

He has read Swinburne and Tennyson and is very sure he won't have anything but "a daughter of the gods, divinely tall, and most divinely fair." Then, of course, there is the "classic profile," the "deep, unfathomable eyes," the "lily-white skin," and "hair like the raven's wing," not to mention the "swan-like neck" and "tapering, shapely fingers."

Mr. Ideal is really a man of refined taste, and the women who hear this impassioned outburst are supremely conscious of their own imperfections.

But beauty is not the only demand of this fastidious gentleman; the fortunate woman whom he deigns to honour must be a paragon of sweetness and docility. No "woman's rights" or "suffrage rant" for him, and none of those high-stepping professional women need apply either—oh, no! And then all of her interests must be his, for of all things on earth, he "does despise a woman with a hobby!" None of these "broad-minded women" were ever intended for Mr. Ideal. He is very certain of that, because away down in his secret heart he was sure he had found the right woman once, but when he did, he learned also that she was somewhat particular about the man she wanted to marry, and the applicant then present did not fill the bill! He is therefore very sure that "a man does not want an intellectual instructor: he wants a wife."

Just like the most of them after all, isn't he?

The year goes round and Mr. Ideal goes away on a summer vacation. There are some pleasant people in the little town to which he goes, and there is a girl in the party with her mother and brother. Mr. Ideal looks her over disapprovingly. She isn't pretty—no, she isn't even good-looking. Her hair is almost red, her eyes are a pale blue, and she wears glasses. Her nose isn't even straight, and it turns up too much besides. Her skin is covered with tiny golden-brown blotches. "Freckles!" exclaims Mr. Ideal, *sotto voce*. Her mouth isn't bad, the lips are red and full and her teeth are white and even. She wears a blue boating suit with an Eton jacket. "So common!" and Mr. Ideal goes away from his secluded point of observation.

A merry laugh reaches his ear, and he turns around. The tall brother is chasing her through the bushes, and she waves a letter tantalisingly at him as she goes, and finally bounds over a low fence and runs across the field, with her big brother in close pursuit. "Hoydenish!" and Mr. Ideal hums softly to himself and goes off to find Smith. Smith is a good fellow and asks Mr. Ideal to go fishing. They go, but don't have a bite, and come home rather cross. Does Smith know the little red-headed girl who was on the piazza this morning?

Yes, he has met her. She has been here about a week. "Rather nice, but not especially attractive, you know." No, she isn't, but he will introduce Mr. Ideal.

Days pass, and Mr. Ideal and Miss Practical are much together. He finds her the jolliest girl he ever knew. She is an enthusiastic advocate of "woman" in every available sphere.

She herself is going to be a trained nurse after she learns to "keep house." "For you know that every woman should be a good housekeeper," she says demurely.

He doesn't exactly like "that trained nurse business," but he admits to himself that, if he were ill, he should like to have Miss Practical smooth his pillow and take care of him.

And so the time goes on, and he is often the companion of the girl. At times, she fairly scintillates with merriment, but she is so dignified, and so womanly—so very careful to keep him at his proper distance—that, well, "she is a type!"

In due course of time, he plans to return to the city, and to the theatres and parties he used to find so pleasant. All his friends are there. No, Miss Practical is not in the city; she is right here. Like a flash a revelation comes over him, and he paces the veranda angrily. Well, there's only one thing to be done— he must tell her about it. Perhaps—and he sees a flash of blue through the shrubbery, which he seeks with the air of a man who has an object in view.

His circle of friends are very much surprised when he introduces Mrs. Ideal, for she is surely different from the ideal woman about whom they have heard so much. They naturally think he is inconsistent, but he isn't, for some subtle alchemy has transfigured the homely little girl into the dearest, best, and altogether most beautiful woman Mr. Ideal has ever seen.

She is domestic in her tastes now, and has abandoned the professional nurse idea. She knows a great deal about Greek and Latin, and still more about Shakespeare and Browning and other authors.

But she neglects neither her books nor her housekeeping, and her husband spends his evenings at home, not because Mrs. Ideal would cry and make a fuss if he didn't, but because his heart is in her keeping, and because his own fireside, with its sweet-faced guardian angel, is to him the most beautiful place on earth, and he has sense enough to appreciate what a noble wife is to him.

The plain truth is, when "any whatsoever" Mr. Ideal loves a woman, he immediately finds her perfect, and transfers to her the attributes which only exist in his imagination. His heart and happiness are there—not with the creatures of his dreams, but the warm, living, loving human being beside him, and to him, henceforth, the ideal is the real.

For "the ideal woman is as gentle as she is strong." She wins her way among her friends and fellow human beings, even though they may be strangers, by doing many a kindness which the most of us are too apt to overlook or ignore.

No heights of thought or feeling are beyond her eager reach, and no human creature has sunk too low for her sympathy and her helping hand. Even the forlorn and friendless dog in the alley looks instinctively into her face for help.

She is in every man's thoughts and always will be, as she always has been—the ideal who shall lead him step by step, and star by star, to the heights which he cannot reach alone.

Ruskin says: "No man ever lived a right life who has not been chastened by a woman's love, strengthened by her courage and guided by her discretion."

The steady flow of the twentieth-century progress has not swept away woman's influence, nor has it crushed out her womanliness. She lives in the hearts of men, a queen as royal as in the days of chivalry, and men shall do and dare for her dear sake as long as time shall last.

The sweet, lovable, loyal woman of the past is not lost; she is only intensified in the brave wifehood and motherhood of our own times. The modern ideal, like that of olden times, is and ever will be, above all things—womanly.

She Is Not Fair

She is not fair to other eyes—
No poet's dream is she,
Nor artist's inspiration, yet
I would not have her be.
She wanders not through princely halls,
A crown upon her hair;
Her heart awaits a single king
Because she is not fair.

Dear lips, your half-shy tenderness
Seems far too much to win!
Yet, has your heart a tiny door
Where I may peep within?
That voiceless chamber, dim and sweet,
I pray may be my own.
Dear little Love, may I come in
And make you mine alone?

She is not fair to other eyes—
I would not have it so;
She needs no further charm or grace
Or aught wealth may bestow;
For when the love light shines and makes
Her dear face glorified—
Ah Sweetheart! queens may come and go
And all the world beside.

The Fin-de-Siècle Woman

The world has fought step by step the elevation of woman from inferiority to equality, but at last she is being recognised as a potent factor in our civilisation.

The most marked change which has been made in woman's position during the last half century or more has been effected by higher education, and since the universities have thrown open their doors to her, she has been allowed, in many cases, to take the same courses that her brother does.

Still, the way has not been entirely smooth for educated and literary women, for the public press has too often frowned upon their efforts to obtain anything like equal recognition for equal ability. The literary woman has, for years, been the target of criticism, and if we are to believe her critics, she has been entirely shunned by the gentlemen of her acquaintance; but the fact that so many of them are wives and mothers, and, moreover, good wives and mothers, proves conclusively that these statements are not trustworthy.

It is true that some prefer the society of women who know just enough to appreciate their compliments—women who deprecate their "strong-minded" sisters, and are ready to agree implicitly with every statement that the lords of creation may make; but this readiness is due to sheer inability to produce a thought of their own.

It is true that some men are afraid of educated women, but a man who is afraid of a woman because she knows something is not the kind of a man she wants to marry. He is not the kind of a man she would choose for either husband or friend; she wants an intellectual companion, and the chances are that she will find him, or rather that he will find her. A woman need not be unwomanly in order to write books that will help the world.

She may be a good housekeeper, even if she does write for the magazines, and the husbands of literary women are not, as some folks would have us believe, neglected and forlorn-looking beings. On the contrary, they carry brave hearts and cheerful faces with them always, since their strength is reinforced by the quiet happiness of their own firesides.

The *fin-de-siècle* woman is literary in one sense, if not in another, for if she may not wield her pen, she can keep in touch with the leading thinkers of the day, and she will prove as pleasant a companion during the long winter evenings as the woman whose husband chose her for beauty and taste in dress.

The literary woman is not slipshod in her apparel, and she may, if she chooses, be a society and club woman as well. Surely there is nothing in literary culture which shall prevent neatness and propriety in dress as well as in conduct.

The devoted admirer of Browning is not liable to quote him in a promiscuous company and though a lady may be familiar with Shakespeare, it does not follow that she will discuss *Hamlet* in social gatherings.

If she reads Greek as readily as she does her mother tongue, you may rest assured she will not mention Homer in ordinary conversation, for a cultivated woman readily recognises the fitness of things, and accords a due deference to the tastes of others. She has her club and her friends, as do the gentlemen of her acquaintance, but her children are not neglected from the fact that she sometimes thinks of other things. She is a helpmeet to her husband, and not a plaything, or a slave. If duty calls her to the kitchen, she goes cheerfully, and, moreover, the cook will not dread to see her coming; or if that important person be absent, the table will be supplied with just as good bread, and just as delicate pastry, as if the lady of the house did not understand the chemicals of their composition.

If trouble comes, she bears it bravely, for the cultured woman has a philosophy which is equal to any emergency, and she does the best she can on all occasions.

If her husband leaves her penniless, she will, if possible, clothe her children with her pen, but if her literary wares are a drug on the market, she will turn bravely to other fields, and find her daily bread made sweet by thankfulness. She does not hesitate to hold out her hands to help a fellow-creature, either man or woman, for she is in all things womanly—a wife to her husband and a mother to her children in the truest sense of the words.

Her knowledge of the classics does not interfere with the making of dainty draperies for her home, and though she may be appointed to read a paper before her club on some scholarly theme, she will listen just as patiently to tales of trouble from childish lips, and will tie up little cut fingers just as sympathetically as her neighbour who folds her arms and who broadly hints that "wimmen's spear is to hum!"

Whether the literary woman be robed in silk and sealskin, or whether she rejoices in the possession of only one best gown, she may, nevertheless, be contented and happy.

Whether she lives in a modest cottage, or in a fashionable home, she may be the same sweet woman, with cheerful face and pleasant voice—with a broad human sympathy which makes her whole life glad.

Be she princess, or Cinderella, she may be still her husband's confidant and cherished friend, to whom he may confide his business troubles and perplexities, certain always of her tender consolation and ready sympathy. She may be quick and versatile, doing well whatever she does at all, for her creed declares that "whatever is honest is honourable."

She glories in her womanhood and has no sympathy with anything which tends to degrade it.

All hail to the woman of the twentieth century; let *fin de siècle* stand for all that is best and noblest in womanhood: for liberty, equality, and fraternity; for right, truth, and justice.

All hail the widespread movement for the higher education of woman, for in intellectual development is the future of posterity, in study is happiness, through the open door of the college is the key of a truer womanhood, a broader humanity, and a brighter hope. In education along the lines of the broadest and wisest culture is to be found the emancipation of the race.

The Moon Maiden

There's a wondrous land of misty gold
Beyond the sunset's bars.
There's a silver boat on a sea of blue,
And the tips of its waves are stars.

And idly rocking to and fro,
Her cloud robes floating by,
There's a maiden fair, with sunny hair,
The queen of the dreamy sky.

Her Son's Wife

The venerable mother-in-law joke appears in the comic papers with astonishing regularity. For a time, perhaps, it may seem to be lost in the mists of oblivion, but even while one is rejoicing at its absence it returns to claim its original position at the head of the procession.

There are two sides to everything, even to an old joke, and the artist always pictures the man's dismay when his wife's mother comes for a visit. Nobody ever sees a drawing of a woman's mother-in-law, and yet, the bitterness and sadness lie mainly there—between the mother and the woman his son has chosen for his wife.

It is a pleasure to believe that the average man is a gentleman, and his inborn respect for his own mother, if nothing else, will usually compel an outward show of politeness to every woman, even though she may be a constant source of irritation. Grey hair has its own claims upon a young man's deference, and, in the business world, he is obliged to learn to hold his tongue, hide his temper, and "assume a virtue though he has it not."

The mother's welcome from her daughter's husband depends much upon herself. Her long years of marriage have been in vain if they have not taught her to watch a man's moods and tenses; when to speak and when to be silent, and how to avoid useless discussion of subjects on which there is a pronounced difference of opinion. Leaving out the personal equation, the older and more experienced woman is better fitted to get along peaceably with a man than the young girl who has her wisdom yet to acquire.

Moreover, it is to the daughter's interest to cement a friendship between her mother and her husband, and so she stands as a shield between the two she holds dearest, to exercise whatever tact she may possess toward an harmonious end.

"A son's a son till he gets him a wife,
But a daughter's a daughter all the days of her life."

Thus the old saying runs, and there is a measure of truth in it, more's the pity. Marriage and a home of her own interfere but little with a daughter's devotion to her mother, even though the daily companionship be materially lessened. The feeling is there and remains unchanged, unless it grows stronger through the new interests on both sides.

If a man has won his wife in spite of her mother's opposition, he can well afford to be gracious and forget the ancient grudge. It is his part, too, to prove to the mother how far she was mistaken, by making the girl who trusted him the happiest wife in the world. The woman who sees her daughter happy will have little against her son-in-law, except that primitive, tribal instinct which survives in most of us, and jealously guards those of our own blood from the aggression of another family or individual.

One may as well admit that a good husband is a very scarce article, and that the mother's anxiety for her daughter is well-founded. No man can escape the sensation of being forever on trial in the eyes of his wife's mother, and woe to him if he makes a mistake or falters in his duty! Things which a woman would gladly condone in her husband are unpardonable sins in the man who has married her daughter, and taken her from a mother's loving care.

A good husband and a good man are not necessarily the same thing. Many a scapegrace has been dearly loved by his wife, and many a highly respected man has been secretly despised by his wife and children. When the prison doors open to discharge the sinners who have served long sentences, the wives of those who have been good husbands are waiting for them with open arms. The others have long since taken advantage of the divorce laws.

Since women know women so well, perhaps it is only natural for a mother to feel that no girl who is good enough for her son ever has been born. All the small deceits, the little schemes and frailties, are as an open book in the eyes of other women.

"If you were a man," said one girl to another, "and knew women as well as you do now, whom would you marry?"

The other girl thought for a moment, and then answered unhesitatingly: "I'd stay single."

Women are always suspicious of each other, and the one who can deceive another woman is entitled to her laurels for cleverness. With the keen insight and quick intuition of the woman on either side of him, when these women are violently opposed to each other, no man need look for peace.

In spite of their discernment, women are sadly deficient in analysis when it comes to a question of self. Neither wife nor mother can clearly see her relation to the man they both love. Blinded by passionate devotion and eager for power, both women lose sight of the truth, and torment themselves and each other with unfounded jealousy and distrust.

In no sense are wife and mother rivals, nor can they ever be so. Neither could take the place of the other for a single instant, and the wife foolishly guards the point where there is no danger, for, of all the women in the world, his mother and sisters are the only ones who could never by any possibility usurp her place.

A woman need only ask herself if she would like to be the mother of her husband—to exchange the love which she now has for filial affection—for a temporary clearness of her troubled skies. The mother need only ask herself if she would surrender her position for the privilege of being her son's wife, if she seeks for light on her dark path.

Yet, in spite of this, the two are often open and acknowledged rivals. A woman recently wrote to the "etiquette department" of a daily paper to know whether she or her son's fiancée should make the first call. In answering the question, the head of the department, who, by the way, has something of a reputation for good sense, wrote as follows: "It is your place to make the first call, and you have my sympathy in your difficult task. You must be brave, for you are going to look into the eyes of a woman whom your son loves better than he does you!" "Better than he does you!" That is where all the trouble lies, for each wishes to be first in a relation where no comparison is possible.

When an American yacht first won the cup, Queen Victoria was watching the race. When she was told that the *America* was in the lead, she asked what boat was second. "Your Majesty," replied the naval officer sadly, "there is no second!"

So, between wife and mother there is no second place, and it is possible for each to own the whole of the loved one's heart, without infringing or even touching upon the rights of the other.

Few of the passengers on a lake steamer, during a trip in northern waters a few years since, will ever forget a certain striking group. Mother and son, and the son's fiancée, were off for a week's vacation. The mother was tall and stately, with snow-white hair and a hard face deeply seamed with wrinkles, and with the fire of southern countries burning in her faded blue eyes. The son was merely a nice boy, with a pleasant face, and the girl, though not pretty, had a fresh look about her which was very attractive.

She wore an engagement ring, so he must have cared for her, but otherwise no one would have suspected it. From beginning to end, his attention was centred upon his mother. He carried his mother's wraps, but the girl carried her own. He talked to the mother, and the girl could speak or not, just as she chose. Never for an instant were the two alone together. They sat on the deck until late at night, with the mother between them. When they changed, the son took his own chair and his mother's, while the girl dragged hers behind them. At the end of their table in the cabin, the mother sat between them at the head. Once, purely by accident, the girl slipped into the nearest chair, which happened to be the mother's, and the deadly silence could be felt even two tables away. The girl turned pale, then the son said: "You'll take the head of the table, won't you, mother?"

The steely tone of her voice could be heard by every one as she said, "No!"

The girl ate little, and soon excused herself to go to her stateroom, but the next day things were as before, and the foolish old mother had her place next to her son.

Discussion was rife among the passengers, till an irreverent youth ended it by saying: "Mamma's got the rocks; that's the why of it!"

Perhaps it was, but one wonders why a man should slight his promised wife so publicly, even to please a mother with "rocks!"

To the mother who adores her son, every girl who smiles at him has matrimonial designs. When he falls in love, it is because he has been entrapped—she seldom considers him as being the aggressive one of the two. The mother of the girl feels the same way, and, in the lower circles, there is occasionally an illuminating time when the two mothers meet.

Each is made aware how the other's offspring has given the entrapped one no peace, and how the affair has been the scandal of two separate neighbourhoods, more eligible partners having been lost by both sides.

In the Declaration of Independence there is no classification of the rights of the married, but the clause regarding "life, liberty, and the pursuit of happiness" has been held pointedly to refer to the matrimonial state. If the mother would accord to her daughter-in-law the same rights she claimed at the outset of her own married life, the relation would be perceptibly smoother in many instances.

When a woman marries, she has a right to expect the love of her husband, material support, a home of her own, even though it be only two tiny rooms, and absolute freedom from outside interference. It is her life, and she must live it in her own way, and a girl of spirit *will* live it in her own way, without taking heed of the consequences, if she is pushed too far.

On the other hand, the mother who bore him still has proprietary rights. She may reasonably claim a share of his society, a part of his earnings, if she needs financial assistance, and his interest in all that nearly concerns her. If she expects to be at the head of his house, with the wife as a sort of a boarder, she need not be surprised if there is trouble.

Marriage brings to a girl certain freedom, but it gives her no superiority to her husband's family. A chain is as strong as its weakest link, and the members of a family do not rise above the general level. Every one of them is as good as the man she has married, and she is not above any of them, unless her own personality commands a higher position.

She treasonably violates the confidence placed in her if she makes a discreditable use of any information coming to her through her association with her husband's family. There are skeletons in every closet, and she may not tell even her own mother of what she has seen in the other house. A single word breathed against her husband's family to an outsider stamps her as a traitor, who deserves a traitor's punishment.

The girl who tells her most intimate friend that the mother of her fiancé "is an old cat," by that act has lowered herself far below the level of any self-respecting cat. Even if outward and visible disgrace comes to the family of her husband, she is unworthy if she does not hold her head high and let the world see her loyalty.

Marriage gives her no right to criticise any member of her husband's family; their faults are out of her reach except by the force of tactful example. Her concern is with herself and him, not his family, and a wise girl, at the beginning of her married life, will draw a sharp line between her affairs and those of others, and will stay on her own side of the line.

When a man falls in love with a thoughtless butterfly, his womenfolk may be pardoned if they stand aghast a moment before they regain their self-command. In a way it is like a guest who is given the freedom of the house, and who, when her visit is over, tells her friends that the parlour carpet was turned, and the stairs left undusted.

Another household is intimately opened to the woman whom the son has married, and the members of it can make no defence. She can betray them if she chooses; there is nothing to shield them except her love for her husband, and too often that is insufficient.

A girl seldom stops to think what she owes to her husband's mother. Twenty-five or thirty years ago, the man she loves was born. Since then there has been no time, sleeping or waking, when he has not been in the thoughts of the mother who has sought to do her best by him. She gave her life wholly to the demands of her child, without a moment's hesitation.

She has sacrificed herself in countless ways, all through those years, in order that he might have his education, his pleasures, and his strong body. With every day he has grown nearer and dearer to her; every day his loss would have been that much harder to bear.

In quiet talks in the twilight, she teaches him to be gentle and considerate, to be courteous to every woman because a woman gave him life; to be brave, noble, and tender; to be strong and fine; to choose honour with a crust, rather than shame with plenty.

Then comes the pretty butterfly, with whom her son is in love. Is it strange that the heart of the mother tightens with sudden pain?

With never a thought, the girl takes it all as her due. She would write a gracious note of thanks to the friend who sent her a pretty handkerchief, but for the woman who is the means of satisfying her heart's desire she has not even toleration. All the sweetness and beauty of his adoring love are a gift to her, unwilling too often, perhaps, but a gift nevertheless, from his mother.

Long years of life have taught the mother what it may mean and what, alas, it does too often mean. Memories only are her portion; she need expect nothing now. He may not come to see his mother for an old familiar talk, because his wife either comes with him, or expects him to be at home. He has no time for his mother's interests or his mother's friends; there is scant welcome in his home for her, because between them has come an alien presence which never yields or softens.

Strangely, and without any definite idea of the change, he comes to see his mother as she is. Once, she was the most beautiful woman in the world, and her roughened hands were lovely because they had toiled for him. Once, her counsel was wise, her judgment good, and the gift of feeling which her motherhood brought her was seen as generous sympathy.

Now, by comparison with a bright, well-dressed wife, he sees what an "old frump" his mother is. She is shabby and old-fashioned, clinging to obsolete forms of speech, hysterical and emotional. When the mists of love have cleared from her boy's eyes, she may just as well give up, because there is no return, save in that other mist which comes too late, when mother is at rest.

The wife who tries to keep alive her husband's love for his family, not only in his heart, but in outward observance as well, serves her own interests even better than theirs. The love of the many comes with the love of the one, and just as truly as he loves his sweetheart better because of his mother and sisters, he may love them better because of her.

The poor heart-hungry mother, who stands by with brimming eyes, fearful that the joy of her life may be taken from her, will be content with but little if she may but keep it for her own. It is only a little while at the longest, for the end of the journey is soon, but sunset and afterglow would have some of the rapture of dawn, if her son's wife opened the door of her young heart and said with true sincerity and wells of tenderness: "Mother—Come!"

A Lullaby

Sleep, baby, sleep,
The twilight breezes blow,
The flower bells are ringing,
The birds are twittering low,
Sleep, baby, sleep.

Sleep, baby, sleep,
The whippoorwill is calling,
The stars are twinkling faintly,
The dew is softly falling,
Sleep, baby, sleep.

Sleep, baby, sleep,
Upon your pillow lying,
The rushes whisper to the stream,
The summer day is dying,
Sleep, baby, sleep.

The Dressing-Sack Habit

Someone has said that a dressing-sack is only a Mother Hubbard with a college education. Accepting this statement as a great truth, one is inclined to wonder whether education has improved the Mother Hubbard, since another clever person has characterised a college as "a place where pebbles are polished and diamonds are dimmed!"

The bond of relationship between the two is not at first apparent, yet there are subtle ties of kinship between the two. If we take a Hubbard and cut it off at the hips, we have only a dressing-sack with a yoke. The dressing-sack, however, cannot be walked on, even when the wearer is stooping, and in this respect it has the advantage of the other; it is also supposed to fit in the back, but it never does.

Doubtless in the wise economy of the universe, where every weed has its function, even this garment has its place—else it would not be.

Possibly one may take a nap, or arrange one's crown of glory to better advantage in a "boudoir négligée," or an invalid may be thus tempted to think of breakfast. Indeed, the habit is apt to begin during illness, when a friend presents the ailing lady with a dainty affair of silk and lace which inclines the suffering soul to frivolities. Presently she sits up, takes notice, and plans more garments of the sort, so that after she fully recovers all the world may see these becoming things!

The worst of the habit is that all the world does see. Fancy runs riot with one pattern, a sewing-machine, and all the remnants a single purse can compass. The lady with a kindly feeling for colour browses along the bargain counter and speedily acquires a rainbow for her own. Each morning she assumes a different phase, and, at the end of the week, one's recollection of her is lost in a kaleidoscopic whirl.

Red, now—is anything prettier than red? And how the men admire it! Does not the dark lady build wisely who dons a red dressing-sack on a cold morning, that her husband may carry a bright bit of colour to the office in his fond memories of home?

A book with a red cover, a red cushion, crimson draperies, and scarlet ribbons, are all notoriously pleasing to monsieur—why not a red dressing-sack?

If questioned, monsieur does not know why, yet gradually his passion for red will wane, then fail. Later in the game, he will be affronted by the colour, even as the gentleman cow in the pasture. It is not the colour, dear madame, but the shiftless garment, which has wrought this change.

There are few who dare to assume pink, for one must have a complexion of peaches and cream, delicately powdered at that, before the rosy hues are becoming. Yet, the sallow lady, with streaks of grey in her hair, crow's feet around her eyes, and little time tracks registered all over her face, will put on a pink dressing-sack when she gets ready for breakfast. She would scream with horror at the thought of a pink and white organdie gown, made over rosy taffeta, but the kimono is another story.

Green dressing-sacks are not often seen, but more's the pity, for in the grand array of colour nothing should be lacking, and the wearers of these garments never seem to stop to think whether or not they are becoming. What could be more cheerful on a cloudy morning than a flannel négligée of the blessed shade of green consecrated to the observance of the seventeenth of March?

It looks as well as many things which are commonly welded into dressing-sacks; then why this invidious distinction?

When we approach blue in our dressing-sack rainbow, speech becomes pitifully weak. Ancient maidens and matrons, with olive skins, proudly assume a turquoise négligée. Blue flannel, with cascades of white lace—could anything be more attractive? It has only one rival—the garment of lavender eiderdown flannel, the button-holes stitched with black yarn, which the elderly widow too often puts on when the tide of her grief has turned.

The combination of black with any shade of purple is well fitted to produce grief, even as the cutting of an onion will bring tears. Could the dear departed see his relict in the morning, with lavender eiderdown environment, he would appreciate his mercies as never before.

The speaking shades of yellow and orange are much affected by German ladies for dressing-sacks, and also for the knitted tippets which our Teutonic friends wear, in and out of the house, from October to July. Canary yellow is delicate and becoming to most, but it is German taste to wear orange.

At first, perhaps, with a sense of the fitness of things, the négligée is worn only in one's own room. She says: "It's so comfortable!" There are degrees in comfort, varying from the easy, perfect fit of one's own skin to a party gown which dazzles envious observers, and why is the adjective reserved for the educated but abbreviated Mother Hubbard?

"The apparel oft proclaims the man," and even more is woman dependent upon her clothes for physical, moral, and intellectual support. An uncorseted body will soon make its influence felt upon the mind. The steel-and-whalebone spine which properly reinforces all feminine vertebra is literally the backbone of a woman's self-respect.

Would the iceman or the janitor hesitate to "talk back" to the uncorseted lady in a pink dressing-sack?—Hardly!

But confront the erring man with a quiet, dignified woman in a crisp shirt-waist and a clean collar—verily he will think twice before he ventures an excuse for his failings.

The iceman and the grocery boy see more dressing-sacks than most others, for they are privileged to approach the back doors of residences, and to hold conversations with the lady of the house, after the departure of him whose duty and pleasure it is to pay for the remnants. And in the lower strata they are known by their clothes.

"Fifty pounds for the red dressing-sack," says the iceman to his helper, "and a hundred for the blue. Step lively now!"

And how should madame know that her order for a steak, a peck of potatoes, and two lemons, is registered in the grocery boy's book under the laconic title, "Pink"?

After breakfast, when she sits down to read the paper and make her plans for the day, the insidious dressing-sack gets in its deadly work.

"I won't dress," she thinks, "until I get ready to go out." After luncheon, she is too tired to go out, and too nearly dead to dress.

Friends come in, perhaps, and say: "Oh, how comfortable you look! Isn't that a dear kimono?" Madame plumes herself with conscious pride, for indeed it is a dear kimono, and already she sees herself with a reputation for "exquisite négligée."

The clock strikes six, and presently the lord of the manor comes home to be fed. "I'm dreadfully sorry, dear, you should find me looking so," says the lady of his heart, "but I just haven't felt well enough to dress. You don't mind, do you?"

The dear, good, subdued soul says he is far from minding, and dinner is like breakfast as far as dressing-sacks go.

Perhaps, in the far depths of his nature, the man wonders why it was that, in the halcyon days of courtship, he never beheld his beloved in the midst of a gunny—no, a dressing-sack. Of course, then, she didn't have to keep house, and didn't have so many cares to tire her. Poor little thing! Perhaps she isn't well!

Isn't she? Let another woman telephone that she has tickets for the matinée, and behold the transformation! Within certain limits and barring severe headaches, a woman is always well enough to do what she wants to do—and no more.

As the habit creeps upon its victim, she loses sight of the fact that there are other clothes. If she has a golf cape, she may venture to go to the letter-box or even to market in her favourite garment. After a while, when the habit is firmly fixed, a woman will wear a dressing-sack all the time—that is, some women will, except on rare and festive occasions. Sometimes in self-defence, she will say that her husband loves soft, fluffy feminine things, and can't bear to see her in a tailor-made outfit. This is why she wears the "soft fluffy things," which, with her, always mean dressing-sacks, all the time he is away from home, as well as when he is there.

It is a mooted question whether shiftlessness causes dressing-sacks, or dressing-sacks cause shiftlessness, but there is no doubt about the loving association of the two. The woman who has nothing to do, and not even a shadow of a purpose in life, will enshrine her helpless back in a dressing-sack. She can't wear corsets, because, forsooth, they "hurt" her. She can't sit at the piano, because it's hard on her back. She can't walk, because she "isn't strong enough." She can't sew, because it makes a pain between her shoulders, and indeed why should she sew when she has plenty of dressing-sacks?

This type of woman always boards, *if she can*, or has plenty of servants at her command, and, in either case, her mind is free to dwell upon her troubles.

First, there is her own weak physical condition. Just wait until she tells you about the last pain she had. She doesn't feel like dressing for dinner, but she will try to wash her face, if you will excuse her! When she returns, she has plucked up enough energy to change her dressing-sack!

The only cure for the habit is a violent measure which few indeed are brave enough to adopt. Make a bonfire of the offensive garments, dear lady; then stay away from the remnant counters, and after a while you will become immune.

Nothing is done in a négligée of this sort which cannot be done equally well in a shirt-waist, crisp and clean, with a collar and belt.

There is a popular delusion to the effect that household tasks require slipshod garments and unkempt hair, but let the frowsy ones contemplate the trained nurse in her spotless uniform, with her snowy cap and apron and her shining hair. Let the doubtful ones go to a cooking school, and see a neat young woman, in a blue gingham gown and a white apron, prepare an eight-course dinner and emerge spotless from the ordeal. We get from life, in most cases, exactly what we put into it. The world is a mirror which gives us smiles or frowns, as we ourselves may choose. The woman who faces the world in a shirt-waist will get shirt-waist appreciation, while for the dressing-sack there is only a slipshod reward.

In the Meadow

The flowers bow their dainty heads,
And see in the shining stream
A vision of sky and silver clouds,
As bright as a fairy's dream.

The great trees nod their sleepy boughs,
The song birds come and go,
And all day long, to the waving ferns
The south wind whispers low.

All day among the blossoms sweet,
The laughing sunbeams play,
And down the stream, in rose-leaf boats
The fairies sail away.

One Woman's Solution of the
Servant Problem

Being a professional woman, my requirements in the way of a housemaid were rather special. While at times I can superintend my small household, and direct my domestic affairs, there are long periods during which I must have absolute quiet, untroubled by door bell, telephone, or the remnants of roast beef.

There are two of us, in a modern six room apartment, in a city where the servant problem has forced a large and ever-increasing percentage of the population into small flats. We have late breakfasts, late dinners, a great deal of company, and an amount of washing, both house and personal, which is best described as "unholy."

Five or six people often drop in informally, and unexpectedly, for the evening, which means, of course, a midnight "spread," and an enormous pile of dishes to be washed in the morning. There are, however, some advantages connected with the situation. We have a laundress besides the maid; we have a twelve-o'clock breakfast on Sunday instead of a dinner, getting the cold lunch ourselves in the evening, thus giving the girl a long afternoon and evening; and we are away from home a great deal, often staying weeks at a time.

The eternal "good wages to right party" of the advertisements was our inducement also, but, apparently, there were no "right parties!"

The previous incumbent, having departed in a fit of temper at half an hour's notice, and left me, so to speak, "in the air," with dinner guests on the horizon a day ahead, I betook myself to an intelligence office, where, strangely enough, there seems to be no intelligence, and grasped the first chance of relief.

Nothing more unpromising could possibly be imagined. The new maid was sad, ugly of countenance, far from strong physically, and in every way hopeless and depressing. She listened, unemotionally, to my glowing description of the situation. Finally she said, "Ay tank Ay try it."

She came, looked us over, worked a part of a week, and announced that she couldn't stay. "Ay can't feel like home here," she said. "Ay am not satisfied."

She had been in her last place for three years, and left because "my's lady, she go to Europe." I persuaded her to try it for a while longer, and gave her an extra afternoon or two off, realising that she must be homesick.

After keeping us on tenter-hooks for two weeks, she sent for her trunk. I discovered that she was a fine laundress, carefully washing and ironing the things which were too fine to go into the regular wash; a most excellent cook, her kitchen and pantry were at all times immaculate; she had no followers, and few friends; meals were ready on the stroke of the hour, and she had the gift of management.

Offset to this was a furious temper, an atmosphere of gloom and depression which permeated the house and made us feel funereal, impertinence of a quality difficult to endure, and the callous, unfeeling, almost inhuman characteristics which often belong in a high degree to the Swedes.

For weeks I debated with myself whether or not I could stand it to have her in the house. I have spent an hour on my own back porch, when I should have been at work, because I was afraid to pass through the room which she happened to be cleaning. Times without number, a crisp muffin, or a pot of perfect coffee, has made me postpone speaking the fateful words which would have separated us. She sighed and groaned and wept at her work, worried about it, and was a fiend incarnate if either of us was five minutes late for dinner. We often hurried through the evening meal so as to leave her free for her evening out, even though I had long since told her not to wash the dishes after dinner, but to pile them neatly in the sink and leave them until morning.

Before long, however, the strictly human side of the problem began to interest me. I had cherished lifelong theories in regard to the brotherhood of man and the uplifting power of personal influence. I had at times been tempted to try settlement work, and here I had a settlement subject in my own kitchen.

There was not a suggestion of fault with the girl's work. She kept her part of the contract, and did it well; but across the wall between us, she glared at—and hated—me.

But, deliberately, I set to work in defence of my theory. I ignored the impertinence, and seemingly did not hear the crash of dishes and the banging of doors. When it came to an issue, I said calmly, though my soul quaked within me: "You are not here to tell me what you will do and what you won't. You are here to carry out my orders, and when you cannot, it is time for you to go."

If she asked me a question about her work which I could not answer offhand, I secretly consulted a standard cook-book, and later gave her the desired information airily. I taught her to cook many of the things which I could cook well, and imbued her with a sort of sneaking respect for my knowledge.

Throughout, I treated her with the perfect courtesy which one lady accords to another, ignoring the impertinence. I took pains to say "please" and "thank you." Many a time I bit my lips tightly against my own rising rage, and afterward in calmness recognised a superior opportunity for self-discipline.

For three or four months, while the beautiful theory wavered in the balance, we fought—not outwardly, but beneath the surface. Daily, I meditated a summary discharge, dissuaded only by an immaculate house and perfectly cooked breakfasts and dinners. I still cherished a lingering belief in personal influence, in spite of the wall which reared itself between us.

A small grey kitten, with wobbly legs and an infantile mew, made the first breach in the wall. She took care of it, loved it, petted it, and began to smile semi-occasionally. She, too, said "please" and "thank you." My husband suggested that we order ten kittens, but I let the good work go on with one, for the time being. Gradually, I learned that the immovable exterior was the natural protection against an abnormal sensitiveness both to praise and blame. Besides the cat, she had two other "weak spots"—an unswerving devotion to a widowed sister with two children, whom she partially supported, and a love for flowers almost pathetic.

As I could, without seeming to make a point of it, I sent things to the sister and the children—partially worn curtains, bits of ribbons, little toys, and the like. I made her room as pretty and dainty as my own, though the furnishings were not so expensive, and gave her a potted plant in a brass jar. When flowers were sent to me, I gave her a few for the vase in her room. She began to say "we" instead of "you." She spoke of "our" spoons, or "our" table linen. She asked, what shall "we" do about this or that? what shall "we" have for dinner? instead of "what do *you* want?" She began to laugh when she played with the kitten, and even to sing at her work.

When she did well, I praised her, as I had all along, but instead of saying, "Iss dat so?" when I remarked that the muffins were delicious or the dessert a great success, her face began to light up, and a smile take the place of the impersonal comment. The furious temper began to wane, or, at least, to be under better control. Guests occasionally inquired, "What have you done to that maid of yours?"

Five times we have left her, for one or two months at a time, on full salary, with unlimited credit at the grocery, and with from fifty to one hundred dollars in cash. During the intervals we heard nothing from her. We have returned each time to an immaculate house, a smiling maid, a perfectly cooked and nicely served meal, and an account correct to a penny, with vouchers to show for it, of the sum with which she had been intrusted.

I noticed each time a vast pride in the fact that she had been so trusted, and from this developed a gratifying loyalty to the establishment. I had told her once to ask her sister and children to spend the day with her while we were gone. It seems that the children were noisy, and the lady in the apartment below us came up to object.

An altercation ensued, ending with a threat from the lady downstairs to "tell Mrs. M. when she came home." Annie told me herself, with flashing eyes and shaking hands. I said, calmly: "The children must have been noisy, or she would not have complained. You are used to them, and besides it would sound worse downstairs than up here. But it doesn't amount to anything, for I had told you you could have the children here, and if I hadn't been able to trust you I wouldn't have left you." Thus the troubled waters were calmed.

The crucial test of her qualities came when I entered upon a long period of exhaustive effort. The first day, we both had a hard time, as her highly specialised Baptist conscience would not permit her to say I was "not at home," when I was merely writing a book. After she thoroughly understood that I was not to be disturbed unless the house took fire, further quiet being insured by disconnecting the doorbell and muffling the telephone, things went swimmingly.

"Annie," I said, "I want you to run this house until I get through with my book. Here is a hundred dollars to start with. Don't let anybody disturb me." She took it with a smile, and a cheerful "all right."

From that moment to the end, I had even less care than I should have had in a well-equipped hotel. Not a sound penetrated my solitude. If I went out for a drink of water, she did not speak to me. We had delicious dinners and dainty breakfasts which might have waited for us, but we never waited a moment for them. She paid herself regularly every Monday morning, kept all receipts, sent out my husband's laundry, kept a strict list of it, mended our clothes, managed our household as economically as I myself could have done it, and, best of all, insured me from any sort of interruption with a sort of fierce loyalty which is beyond any money value.

Once I overheard a colloquy at my front door, which was briefly and decisively terminated thus: "Ay already tell you dat you *not see her*! She says to me, 'Annie, you keep dose peoples off from me,' and Ay *keep dem off*!" I never have known what dear friend was thus turned away from my inhospitable door.

Fully appreciating my blessings, the night I finished my work I went into the kitchen with a crisp, new, five-dollar bill. "Annie," I said, "here is a little extra money for you. You've been so nice about the house while I've been busy."

She opened her eyes wide, and stared. "You don't have to do dat," she said.

"I know I don't," I laughed, "but I like to do it."

"You don't have to do dat," she repeated. "Ay like to do de housekeeping."

"I know," I said again, "and I like to do this. You've done lots of things for me you didn't have to do. Why shouldn't I do something for you?"

At that she took it, offering me a rough wet hand, which I took gravely. "Tank you," she said, and the tears rolled down her cheeks.

"You've earned it," I assured her, "and you deserve it, and I'm very glad I can give it to you."

From that hour she has been welded to me in a bond which I fondly hope is indestructible. She laughs and sings at her work, pets her beloved kitten, and diffuses through my six rooms the atmosphere of good cheer. She "looks after me," anticipates my wishes, and dedicates to me a continual loyal service which has no equivalent in dollars and cents. She asked me, hesitatingly, if she might not get some one to fill her place for three months while she went back to Sweden. I didn't like the idea, but I recognised her well-defined right.

"Ay not go," she said, "if you not want me to. Ay tell my sister dat I want to stay wid Mrs. M. until she send me away."

I knew she would have to go some time before she settled down to perpetual residence in an alien land, so I bade her God-speed. She secured the substitute and instructed her, arranged the matter of wages, and vouched for her honesty, but not for her work.

Before she left the city, I found that the substitute was hopelessly incompetent and stupid. When Annie came to say "good-bye" to me, I told her about the new girl. She broke down and wept. "Ay sorry Ay try to go," she sobbed. "Ay tell my sister dere iss nobody what can take care of Mrs. M. lak Ay do!"

I was quite willing to agree with her, but I managed to dry her tears. Discovering that she expected to spend two nights in a day coach, and remembering one dreadful night when I could get no berth, I gave her the money for a sleeping-car ticket both ways, as a farewell gift. The tears broke forth afresh. "You been so good to me and to my sister," she sobbed. "Ay can't never forget dat!"

"Cheer up," I answered, wiping the mist from my own eyes. "Go on, and have the best time you ever had in your life, and don't worry about me—I'll get along somehow. And if you need money while you are away, write to me, and I'll send you whatever you need. We'll fix it up afterward."

Once again she looked at me, with the strangest look I have ever seen on the human face.

"Tank you," she said slowly. "Dere iss not many ladies would say dat."

"Perhaps not," I replied, "but, remember, Annie, I can trust you."

"Yes," she cried, her face illumined as by some great inward light, "you can trust me!"

I do not think she loves us yet, but I believe in time she will.

The day the new girl came, I happened to overhear a much valued reference to myself: "Honestly," she said, "Ay been here more dan one year, and Ay never hear a wrong word between her and him, nor between her and me. It's shust wonderful. Ay isn't been see anyting like it since Ay been in diss country."

"Is it so wonderful?" I asked myself, as I stole away, my own heart aglow with the consciousness of a moral victory, "and is the lack of self-control and human kindness at the bottom of the American servant problem? Are we women such children that we cannot deal wisely with our intellectual inferiors?" And more than all I had given her, as I realised then for the first time, was the power of self-discipline and self-control which she, all unknowingly, had developed in me.

I have not ceased the "treatment," even though the patient is nearly well. It costs me nothing to praise her when she deserves it, to take an occasional friend into her immaculate kitchen, and to show the shining white pantry shelves (without papers), while she blushes and smiles with pleasure. It costs me nothing to see that she overhears me while I tell a friend over the telephone how capable she has been during the stress of my work, or how clean the house is when we come home after a long absence. It costs me nothing to send her out for a walk, or a visit to a nearby friend, on the afternoons when her work is finished and I am to be at home—nothing to call her attention to a beautiful sunset or a perfect day, or to tell her some amusing story that her simple mind can appreciate. It costs me nothing to tell her how well she looks in her cap and apron (only I call the cap a "hair-bow"), nor that one of the guests said she made the best cake she had ever eaten in her life.

It costs me little to give her a pretty hatpin, or some other girlish trifle at Easter, to bring her some souvenir of our travels, to give her a fresh ribbon for her belt from my bolt, or some little toy "for de children."

It means only a thought to say when she goes out, "Good-bye! Have a good time!" or to say when I go out, "Good-bye! Be good!" It means little to me to tell her how much my husband or our guests have enjoyed the dinner, or to have him go into the kitchen sometimes, while she is surrounded by a mountain of dishes, with a cheery word and a fifty-cent piece.

It isn't much out of my way to do a bit of shopping for her when I am shopping for myself, and no trouble at all to plan for her new gowns, or to tell her that her new hat is very pretty and becoming.

When her temper gets the better of her these days, I can laugh her out of it. "To think," I said once, "of a fine, capable girl like you flying into a rage because some one has borrowed your clothesline without asking for it!"

The clouds vanished with a smile. "Dat iss funny of me," she said.

When her work goes wrong, as of course it sometimes does, though rarely, and she is worrying for fear I shall be displeased, I say: "Never mind, Annie; things don't always go right for any of us. Don't worry about it, but be careful next time."

It has cost me time and effort and money, and an infinite amount of patience and tact, not to mention steady warfare with myself, but in return, what have I? A housemaid, as nearly perfect, perhaps, as they can ever be on this faulty earth, permanently in my service, as I hope and believe.

If any one offers her higher wages, I shall meet the "bid," for she is worth as much to me as she can be to any one else. Besides giving me superior service, she has done me a vast amount of good in furnishing me the needed material for the development of my character.

On her own ground, she respects my superior knowledge. Once or twice I have heard her say of some friend, "Her's lady, she know nodding at all about de housekeeping—no, nodding at all!"

The airy contempt of the tone is quite impossible to describe.

A neighbour whom she assisted in a time of domestic stress, during my absence, told me amusedly of her reception in her own kitchen. "You don't have to come all de time to de kitchen to tell me," remarked Annie.

"Doesn't Mrs. M. do that?" queried my neighbour, lightly.

"Ay should say not," returned the capable one, indignantly. "She nefer come in de kitchen, and *she know, too*!"

While that was not literally true, because I do go into my kitchen if I want to, and cook there if I like, I make a point of not intruding. She knows what she is to do, and I leave her to do it, in peace and comfort.

Briefly summarised, the solution from my point of view is this. *Know her work yourself, down to the last detail;* pay the wages which other people would be glad to pay for the same service; keep your temper, and, in the face of everything, *be kind!* Remember that housework is hard work—that it never stays done—that a meal which it takes half a day to prepare is disposed of in half an hour. Remember, too, that it requires much intelligence and good judgment to be a good cook, and that the daily tasks lack inspiration. The hardest part of housework must be done at a time when many other people are free for rest and enjoyment, and it carries with it a social bar sinister when it is done for money. The woman who does it for her board and clothes, in her own kitchen, does not necessarily lose caste, but doing it for a higher wage, in another's kitchen, makes one almost an outcast. Strange and unreasonable, but true.

It was at my own suggestion that she began to leave the dishes piled up in the sink until morning. When the room is otherwise immaculate, a tray of neatly piled plates, even if unwashed, does not disturb my æsthetic sense.

Ordinarily, she is free for the evening at half-past seven or a quarter of eight—always by eight. Her evenings are hers, not mine,—unless I pay her extra, as I always do. A dollar or so counts for nothing in the expense of an entertainment, and she both earns and deserves the extra wage.

If I am to entertain twenty or thirty people—the house will hold no more, and I cannot ask more than ten to dinner—I consult with her, decide upon the menu, tell her that she can have all the help she needs, and go my ways in peace. I can order the flowers, decorate the table, put on my best gown, and receive my guests, unwearied, with an easy mind.

When I am not expecting guests, I can leave the house immediately after breakfast, without a word about dinner, and return to the right sort of a meal at seven o'clock, bringing a guest or two with me, if I telephone first.

I can work for six weeks or two months in a seclusion as perfect as I could have in the Sahara Desert, and my household, meanwhile, will move as if on greased skids. I can go away for two months and hear nothing from her, and yet know that everything is all right at home. I think no more about it, so far as responsibility is concerned, when I am travelling, than as if I had no home at all. When we leave the apartment alone in the evening, we turn on the most of the lights, being assured by the police that burglars will never molest a brilliantly illuminated house.

The morose countenance of my ugly maid has subtly changed. It radiates, in its own way, beauty and good cheer. Her harsh voice is gentle, her manner is kind, her tastes are becoming refined, her ways are those of a lady.

My friends and neighbours continually allude to the transformation as "a miracle." The janitor remarked, in a burst of confidence, that he "never saw anybody change so." He "reckoned," too, that "it must be the folks she lives with!" Annie herself, conscious of a change, recently said complacently: "Ay guess Ay wass one awful crank when Ay first come here."

And so it happens that the highest satisfaction is connected with the beautiful theory, triumphantly proven now, against heavy odds. Whatever else I may have done, I have taught one woman the workman's pride in her work, shown her where true happiness lies, and set her feet firmly on the path of right and joyous living.

To a Violin

(Antonius Stradivarius, 1685.)

What flights of years have gone to fashion thee,
My violin! What centuries have wrought
Thy sounding fibres! What dead fingers taught
Thy music to awake in ecstasy
Beyond our human dreams? Thy melody
Is resurrection. Every buried thought
Of singing bird, or stream, or south wind, fraught
With tender message, or of sobbing sea,
Lives once again. The tempest's solemn roll
Is in thy passion sleeping, till the king
Whose touch is mastery shall sound thy soul.
The organ tones of ocean shalt thou bring,
The crashing chords of thunder, and the whole
Vast harmony of God. Ah, Spirit, sing!

The Old Maid

One of the best things the last century has done for woman is to make single-blessedness appear very tolerable indeed, even if it be not actually desirable.

The woman who didn't marry used to be looked down upon as a sort of a "leftover" without a thought, apparently, that she may have refused many a chance to change her attitude toward the world. But now, the "bachelor maid" is welcomed everywhere, and is not considered eccentric on account of her oneness.

With the long records of the divorce courts before their eyes, it is not very unusual for the younger generation of women nowadays deliberately to choose spinsterhood as their independent lot in life.

A girl said the other day: "It's no use to say that a woman can't marry if she wants to. Look around you, and see the women who *have* married, and then ask yourself if there is anybody who can't!"

This is a great truth very concisely stated. It is safe to say that no woman ever reached twenty-five years of age, and very few have passed twenty, without having an opportunity to become somebody's mate.

A very small maiden with very bright eyes once came to her mother with the question: "Mamma, do you think I shall ever have a chance to get married?"

And the mother answered: "Surely you will, my child; the woods are full of offers of marriage—no woman can avoid them."

And ere many years had passed the maiden had learned that the wisdom of her mother's prophecy was fully vindicated.

Every one knows that a woman needs neither beauty, talent, nor money to win the deepest and sincerest love that man is capable of giving.

Single life is, with rare exceptions, a matter of choice and not of necessity; and while it is true that a happy married life is the happiest position for either man or woman, there are many things which are infinitely worse than being an old maid, and chiefest among these is marrying the wrong man!

The modern woman looks her future squarely in the face and decides according to her best light whether her happiness depends upon spinsterhood or matrimony. This decision is of course influenced very largely by the quality of her chances in either direction, but if the one whom she fully believes to be the right man comes along, he is likely to be able to overcome strong objections to the married state. If love comes to her from the right source, she takes it gladly; otherwise she bravely goes her way alone, often showing the world that some of the most mother-hearted women are not really mothers. Think of the magnificent solitude of such women as Florence Nightingale and our own splendid Frances Willard! Who shall say that these, and thousands of others of earth's grandest souls, were not better for their single-heartedness in the service of humanity?

A writer in a leading journal recently said: "The fact that a woman remains single is a tribute to her perception. She gains an added dignity from being hard to suit."

This, from the pen of a man, is somewhat of a revelation, in the light of various masculine criticisms concerning superfluous women. No woman is superfluous. God made her, and put her into this world to help her fellow-beings. There is a little niche somewhere which she, and she alone, can fill. She finds her own completeness in rounding out the lives of others.

It has been said that the average man may be piloted through life by one woman, but it must be admitted that several of him need somewhere near a dozen of the fair sex to wait upon him at the same time. His wife and mother are kept "hustling," while his "sisters and his aunts" are likely to be "on the keen jump" from the time his lordship enters the house until he leaves it!

But to return to the "superfluous woman,"—although we cannot literally return to her because she does not exist. Of the "old maid" of to-day, it is safe to say that she has her allotted plane of usefulness. She isn't the type our newspaper brethren delight to caricature. She doesn't dwell altogether upon the subject of "woman's sphere," which, by the way, comes very near being the plane of the earth's sphere, and she need not, for her position is now well recognised.

She doesn't wear corkscrew curls and hideous reform garments. She is a dainty, feminine, broad-minded woman, and a charming companion. Men are her friends, and often her lovers, in her old age as well as in her youth.

Every old maid has her love story, a little romance that makes her heart young again as she dreams it over in the firelight, and it calls a happy smile to the faded face.

Or, perhaps, it is the old, sad story of a faithless lover, or a happiness spoiled by gossips—or it may be the scarcely less sad story of love and death.

Ibsen makes two of his characters, a young man and woman who love each other, part voluntarily on the top of a high mountain in order that they may be enabled to keep their high ideals and uplifting love for each other.

So the old maid keeps her ideals, not through fulfilment, but through memory, and she is far happier than many a woman who finds her ideal surprisingly and disagreeably real.

The bachelor girl and the bachelor man are much on the increase. Marriage is not in itself a failure, but the people who enter unwisely into this solemn covenant too often are not only failures, but bitter disappointments to those who love them best.

Life for men and women means the highest usefulness and happiness, for the terms are synonymous, neither being able to exist without the other.

The model spinster of to-day is philanthropic. She is connected, not with innumerable charities, but with a few well-chosen ones. She gives freely of her time and money in many ways, where her left hand scarcely knoweth what her right doeth, and the record of her good works is not found in the chronicles of the world.

She is literary, musical, or artistic. She is a devoted and loyal club member, and is well informed on the leading topics of the day, while the resources of her well-balanced mind are always at the service of her friends.

And when all is said and done, the highest and truest life is within the reach of us all. Doing well whatever is given us to do will keep us all busy, and married or single, no woman has a right to be idle. The old maid may be womanly and mother-hearted as well as the wife and mother.

The Spinster's Rubaiyat

I

Wake! For the hour of hope will soon take flight
And on your form and features leave a blight;
Since Time, who heals full many an open wound,
More oft than not is impolite.

II

Before my relatives began to chide,
Methought the voice of conscience said inside:
"Why should you want a husband, when you have
A cat who seldom will at home abide?"

III

And, when the evening breeze comes in the door,
The lamp smokes like a chimney, only more;
And yet the deacon of the church
Is telling every one my parrot swore.

IV

Behold, my aunt into my years inquires,
Then swiftly with my parents she conspires,
And in the family record changes dates—
In that same book that says all men are liars.

V

Come, fill the cup and let the kettle sing!
What though upon my finger gleams no ring,
Save that cheap turquoise that I bought myself?
The coming years a gladsome change may bring.

VI

Here, minion, fill the steaming cup that clears
The skin I will not have exposed to jeers,
And rub this wrinkle vigorously until
The maddening crow's-foot wholly disappears.

VII

And let me don some artificial bloom,
And turn the lamps down low, and make a gloom

That spreads from library to hall and stair;
Thus do I look my best—but ah, for whom?

The Rights of Dogs

We hear a great deal about the "rights of men" and still more, perhaps, about the "rights of women," but few stop to consider those which properly belong to the friend and companion of both—the dog.

According to our municipal code, a dog must be muzzled from June 1st to September 30th. The wise men who framed this measure either did not know, or did not stop to consider, that a dog perspires and "cools off" only at his mouth.

Man and the horse have tiny pores distributed all over the body, but in the dog they are found only in the tongue.

Any one who has had a fever need not be told what happened when these pores ceased to act; what, then, must be the sufferings of a dog on a hot day, when, securely muzzled, he takes his daily exercise?

Even on the coolest days, the barbarous muzzle will fret a thoroughbred almost to insanity, unless, indeed, he has brains to free himself, as did a brilliant Irish setter which we once knew. This wise dog would run far ahead of his human guardian, and with the help of his forepaws slip the strap over his slender head, then hide the offending muzzle in the gutter, and race onward again. When the loss was discovered, it was far too late to remedy it by any search that could be instituted.

And still, without this uncomfortable encumbrance, it is unsafe for any valuable dog to be seen, even on his own doorsteps, for the "dog-catcher" is ever on the look-out for blue-blooded victims.

The homeless mongrel, to whom a painless death would be a blessing, is left to get a precarious living as best he may from the garbage boxes, and spread pestilence from house to house, but the setter, the collie, and the St. Bernard are choked into insensibility with a wire noose, hurled into a stuffy cage, and with the thermometer at ninety in the shade, are dragged through the blistering city, as a sop to that Cerberus of the law which demands for its citizens safety from dogs, and pays no attention to the lawlessness of men.

The dog tax which is paid every year is sufficient to guarantee the interest of the owner in his dog. Howells has pitied "the dogless man," and Thomas Nelson Page has said somewhere that "some of us know what it is to be loved by a dog."

Countless writers have paid tribute to his fidelity and devotion, and to the constant forgiveness of blows and neglect which spring from the heart of the commonest cur.

The trained hunter, who is as truly a sportsman as the man who brings down the birds he finds, can be easily fretted into madness by the injudicious application of the muzzle.

The average dog is a gentleman and does not attack people for the pleasure of it, and it is lamentably true that people who live in cities often find it necessary to keep some sort of a dog as a guardian to life and property. In spite of his loyalty, which every one admits, the dog is an absolute slave. Men with less sense, and less morality, constitute a court from which he has no appeal.

Four or five years of devotion to his master's interests, and four or five years of peaceful, friendly conduct, count for absolutely nothing beside the perjured statement of some man, or even woman, who, from spite against the owner, is willing to assert, "the dog is vicious."

"He is very imprudent, a dog is," said Jerome K. Jerome. "He never makes it his business to inquire whether you are in the right or wrong—never bothers as to whether you are going up or down life's ladder—never asks whether you are rich or poor, silly or wise, saint or sinner. You are his pal. That is enough for him, and come luck or misfortune, good repute or bad, honour or shame, he is going to stick to you, to comfort you, guard you, and give his life for you, if need be—foolish, brainless, soulless dog!

"Ah! staunch old friend, with your deep, clear eyes, and bright quick glances that take in all one has to say, before one has time to speak it, do you know you are only an animal and have no mind?

"Do you know that dull-eyed, gin-sodden lout leaning against the post out there is immeasurably your intellectual superior? Do you know that every little-minded selfish scoundrel, who never had a thought that was not mean and base—whose every action is a fraud and whose every utterance is a lie; do you know that these are as much superior to you as the sun is to the rush-light, you honourable, brave-hearted, unselfish brute?

"They are men, you know, and men are the greatest, noblest, wisest, and best beings in the universe. Any man will tell you that."

Are the men whom we elect to public office our masters or our servants? If the former, let us change our form of government; if the latter, let us hope that from somewhere a little light may penetrate their craniums and that they may be induced to give the dog a chance.

Twilight

The birds were hushed into silence,
The clouds had sunk from sight,
And the great trees bowed to the summer breeze
That kissed the flowers good-night.

The stars came out in the cool still air,
From the mansions of the blest,
And softly, over the dim blue hills,
Night came to the world with rest.

Women's Clothes in Men's Books

When asked why women wrote better novels than men, Mr. Richard Le Gallienne is said to have replied, more or less conclusively, "They don't"; thus recalling *Punch's* famous advice to those about to marry.

Happily there is no segregation in literature, and masculine and feminine hands alike may dabble in fiction, as long as the publishers are willing.

If we accept Zola's dictum to the effect that art is nature seen through the medium of a temperament, the thing is possible to many, though the achievement may differ both in manner and degree. For women have temperament—too much of it—as the hysterical novelists daily testify.

The gentleman novelist, however, prances in boldly, where feminine feet well may fear to tread, and consequently has a wider scope for his writing. It is not for a woman to mingle in a barroom brawl and write of the thing as she sees it. The prize-ring, the interior of a cattle-ship, Broadway at four in the morning—these and countless other places are forbidden by her innate refinement as well as by the Ladies' Own, and all the other aunties who have taken upon themselves the guardianship of the Home with a big H.

Fancy the outpouring of scorn upon the luckless offender's head if one should write to the Manners and Morals Department of the Ladies' Own as follows: "Would it be proper for a lady novelist, in search of local colour and new experiences, to accept the escort of a strange man at midnight if he was too drunk to recognise her afterward?" Yet a man in the same circumstances would not hesitate to put an intoxicated woman into a sea-going cab, and would plume himself for a year and a day upon his virtuous performance.

All things are considered proper for a man who is about to write a book. Like the disciple of Mary McLane who stole a horse in order to get the emotions of a police court, he may delve deeply not only into life, but into that under-stratum which is not spoken of, where respectable journals circulate.

Everything is fish that comes into his net. If conscientious, he may even undertake marriage in order to study the feminine personal equations at close range. Woman's emotions, singly and collectively, are pilloried before his scientific gaze. He cowers before one problem, and one only—woman's clothes!

Carlyle, after long and painful thought, arrives at the conclusion that "cut betokens intellect and talent; colour reveals temper and heart."

This reminds one of the language of flowers, and the directions given for postage-stamp flirtation. If that massive mind had penetrated further into the mysteries of the subject, we might have been told that a turnover collar indicated that the woman was a High Church Episcopalian who had embroidered two altar cloths, and that suède gloves show a yielding but contradictory nature.

Clothes are, undoubtedly, indices of character and taste, as well as a sop to conventionality, but this only when one has the wherewithal to browse at will in the department store. Many a woman with ermine tastes has only a rabbit-fur pocket-book, and thus her clothes wrong her in the sight of gods and women, though men know nothing about it.

Once upon a time there was a notion to the effect that women dressed to please men, but that idea has long since been relegated to the limbo of forgotten things.

Not one man in a thousand can tell the difference between Brussels point at thirty dollars a yard, and imitation Valenciennes at ten or fifteen cents a yard which was one of the "famous Friday features in the busy bargain basement."

But across the room, yea, even from across the street, the eagle eye of another woman can unerringly locate the Brussels point and the mock Valenciennes.

A man knows silk by the sound of it and diamonds by the shine. He will say that his heroine "was richly dressed in silk." Little does he wot of the difference between taffeta at eighty-five cents a yard and broadcloth at four dollars. Still less does he know that a white cotton shirt-waist represents financial ease, and a silk waist of festive colouring represents poverty, since it takes but two days to "do up" a white shirt-waist in one sense, and thirty or forty cents to do it up in the other!

One listens with wicked delight to men's discourse upon woman's clothes. Now and then a man will express his preference for a tailored gown, as being eminently simple and satisfactory. Unless he is married and has seen the bills for tailored gowns, he also thinks they are inexpensive.

It is the benedict, wise with the acquired knowledge of the serpent, who begs his wife to get a new party gown and let the tailor-made go until next season. He also knows that when the material is bought, the expense has scarcely begun, whereas the ignorant bachelor thinks that the worst is happily over.

In *A Little Journey through the World* Mr. Warner philosophised thus: "How a woman in a crisis hesitates before her wardrobe, and at last chooses just what will express her innermost feelings!"

If all a woman's feelings were to be expressed by her clothes, the benedicts would immediately encounter financial shipwreck. On account of the lamentable scarcity of money and closets, one is eternally adjusting the emotion to the gown.

Some gown, seen at the exact psychological moment, fixes forever in a man's mind his ideal garment. Thus we read of blue calico, of pink-and-white print, and more often still, of white lawn. Mad colour combinations run riot in the masculine fancy, as in the case of a man who boldly described his favourite costume as "red, with black ruffles down the front!"

Of a hat, a man may be a surpassingly fine critic, since he recks not of style. Guileful is the woman who leads her liege to the millinery and lets him choose, taking no heed of the price and the attendant shock until later.

A normal man is anxious that his wife shall be well dressed because it shows the critical observer that his business is a great success. After futile explorations in the labyrinth, he concerns himself simply with the fit, preferring always that the clothes of his heart's dearest shall cling to her as lovingly as a kid glove, regardless of the pouches and fulnesses prescribed by Dame Fashion.

In the writing of books, men are at their wits' end when it comes to women's clothes. They are hampered by no restrictions—no thought of style or period enters into their calculations, and unless they have a wholesome fear of the unknown theme, they produce results which further international gaiety.

Many an outrageous garment has been embalmed in a man's book, simply because an attractive woman once wore something like it when she fed the novelist. Unbalanced by the joy of the situation, he did not accurately observe the garb of the ministering angel, and hence we read of "a clinging white gown" in the days of stiff silks and rampant crinoline; of "the curve of the upper arm" when it took five yards for a pair of sleeves, and of "short walking skirts" during the reign of bustles and trains!

In *The Blazed Trail*, Mr. White observes that his heroine was clad in brown which fitted her slender figure perfectly. As Hilda had yellow hair, "like corn silk," this was all right, and if the brown was of the proper golden shade, she was doubtless stunning when Thorpe first saw her in the forest. But the gown could not have fitted her as the sheath encases the dagger, for before the straight-front corsets there were the big sleeves, and still further back were bustles and *bouffant* draperies. One does not get the impression that *The Blazed Trail* was placed in the days of crinolines, but doubtless Hilda's clothes did not fit as Mr. White seems to think they did.

That strenuous follower of millinery, Mr. Gibson, might give lessons to his friend, Mr. Davis, with advantage to the writer, if not to the artist. In *Captain Macklin*, the young man's cousin makes her first appearance in a thin gown, and a white hat trimmed with roses, reminding the adventurous captain of a Dresden statuette, in spite of the fact that she wore heavy gauntlet gloves and carried a trowel. The lady had been doing a hard day's work in the garden. No woman outside the asylum ever did gardening in such a costume, and Mr. Davis evidently has the hat and gown sadly mixed with some other pleasant impression.

The feminine reader immediately hides Mr. Davis' mistake with the broad mantle of charity, and in her own mind clothes Beatrice properly in a short walking skirt, heavy shoes, shirt-waist, old hat tied down over the ears with a rumpled ribbon, and a pair of ancient masculine gloves, long since discarded by their rightful owner. Thus does lovely woman garden, except on the stage and in men's books.

In *The Story of Eva*, Mr. Payne announces that Eva climbed out of a cab in "a fawn-coloured jacket," conspicuous by reason of its newness, and a hat "with an owl's head upon it!"

The jacket was possibly a coat of tan covert cloth with strapped seams, but it is the startling climax which claims attention. An owl! Surely not, Mr. Payne! It may have been a parrot, for once upon a time, before the Audubon Society met with widespread recognition, women wore such things, and at afternoon teas where many fair ones were gathered together the parrot garniture was not without significance. But an owl's face, with its glaring glassy eyes, is too much like a pussy cat's to be appropriate, and one could not wear it at the back without conveying an unpleasant impression of two-facedness, if the coined word be permissible.

Still the owl is no worse than the trimming suggested by a funny paper. The tears of mirth come yet at the picture of a hat of rough straw, shaped like a nest, on which sat a full-fledged Plymouth Rock hen, with her neck proudly, yet graciously curved. Perhaps Mr. Payne saw the picture and forthwith decided to do something in the same line, but there is a singular inappropriateness in placing the bird of Minerva upon the head of poor Eva, who made the old, old bargain in which she had everything to lose, and nothing save the bitterest experience to gain. A stuffed kitten, so young and innocent that its eyes were still blue and bleary, would have been more appropriate on Eva's bonnet, and just as pretty.

In *The Fortunes of Oliver Horn*, Margaret Grant wears a particularly striking costume:

"The cloth skirt came to her ankles, which were covered with yarn stockings, and her feet were encased in shoes that gave him the shivers, the soles being as thick as his own and the leather as tough.

"Her blouse was of grey flannel, belted to the waist by a cotton saddle-girth, white and red, and as broad as her hand. The tam-o-shanter was coarse and rough, evidently home-made, and not at all like McFudd's, which was as soft as the back of a kitten and without a seam."

With all due respect to Mr. Smith, one must insist that Margaret's shoes were all right as regards material and build. She would have been more comfortable if they had been "high-necked" shoes, and, in that case, the yarn hosiery would not have troubled him, but that is a minor detail. The quibble comes at the belt, and knowing that Margaret was an artist, we must be sure that Mr. Smith was mistaken. It may have been one of the woven cotton belts, not more than two inches wide, which, for a dizzy moment, were at the height of fashion, and then tottered and fell, but a "saddle-girth"—never!

In that charming morceau, *The Inn of the Silver Moon*, Mr. Viele puts his heroine into plaid stockings and green knickerbockers—an outrageous costume truly, even for wheeling.

As if recognising his error, and, with veritable masculine stubbornness, refusing to admit it, Mr. Viele goes on to say that the knickerbockers were "tailor-made!" And thereby he makes a bad matter very much worse.

In *The Wings of the Morning*, Iris, in spite of the storm through which the *Sirdar* vainly attempts to make its way, appears throughout in a "lawn dress"— white, undoubtedly, since all sorts and conditions of men profess to admire white lawn!

How cold the poor girl must have been! And even if she could have been so inappropriately gowned on shipboard, she had plenty of time to put on a warm and suitable tailor-made gown before she was shipwrecked. This is sheer fatuity, for any one with Mr. Tracy's abundant ingenuity could easily have contrived ruin for the tailored gown in time for Iris to assume masculine garb and participate bravely in that fearful fight on the ledge.

Whence, oh whence, comes this fondness for lawn? Are not organdies, dimities, and embroidered muslins fully as becoming to the women who trip daintily through the pages of men's books? Lawn has been a back number for many a weary moon, and still we read of it!

"When in doubt, lead trumps," might well be paraphrased thus: "When in doubt, put her into white lawn!" Even "J. P. M.," that gentle spirit to whom so many hidden things were revealed, sent his shrewish "Kate" off for a canter through the woods in a white gown, and, if memory serves, it was lawn!

In *The Master*, Mr. Zangwill describes Eleanor Wyndwood as "the radiant apparition of a beautiful woman in a shimmering amber gown, from which her shoulders rose dazzling."

So far so good. But a page or two farther on, that delightful minx, Olive Regan, wears "a dress of soft green-blue cut high, with yellow roses at the throat." One wonders whether Mr. Zangwill ever really saw a woman in any kind of a gown "with yellow roses at the throat," or whether it is but the slip of an overstrained fancy. The fact that he has married since writing this gives a goodly assurance that by this time he knows considerably more about gowns.

Still there is always a chance that the charm may not work, for Mr. Arthur Stringer, who has been reported as being married to a very lovely woman, takes astonishing liberties in *The Silver Poppy*:

"She floated in before Reppellier, buoyant, smiling, like a breath of open morning itself, a confusion of mellow autumnal colours in her wine-coloured gown, and a hat of roses and mottled leaves.

"Before she had as much as drawn off her gloves—and they were always the most spotless of white gloves—she glanced about in mock dismay, and saw that the last of the righting up had already been done."

Later, we read that the artist pinned an American Beauty upon her gown, then shook his head over the colour combination and took it off. If the American Beauty jarred enough for a man to notice it, the dress must have been the colour of claret, or Burgundy, rather than the clear soft gold of sauterne.

This brings us up with a short turn before the hat. What colour were the roses? Surely they were not American Beauties, and they could not have been pink. Yellow roses would have been a fright, so they must have been white ones, and a hat covered with white roses is altogether too festive to wear in the morning. The white gloves also would have been sadly out of place.

What a comfort it would be to all concerned if the feminine reader could take poor Cordelia one side and fix her up a bit! One could pat the artistic disorder out of her beautiful yellow hair, help her out of her hideous clothes into a grey tailor-made, with a shirt-waist of mercerised white cheviot, put on a stock of the same material, give her a "ready-to-wear" hat of the same trig-tailored quality, and, as she passed out, hand her a pair of grey suède gloves which exactly matched her gown.

Though grey would be more becoming, she might wear tan as a concession to Mr. Stringer, who evidently likes yellow.

In the same book, we find a woman who gathers up her "yellow skirts" and goes down a ladder. It might have been only a yellow taffeta drop-skirt under tan etamine, but we must take his word for it, as we did not see it and he did.

As the Chinese keep the rat tails for the end of the feast, the worst clothes to be found in any book must come last by way of climax. Mr. Dixon, in *The Leopard's Spots*, has easily outdone every other knight of the pen who has entered the lists to portray women's clothes. Listen to the inspired description of Miss Sallie's gown!

"She was dressed in a morning gown of a soft red material, trimmed with old cream lace. The material of a woman's dress had never interested him before. He knew calico from silk, but beyond that he never ventured an opinion. To colour alone he was responsive. This combination of red and creamy white, *with the bodice cut low, showing the lines of her beautiful white shoulders*, and the great mass of dark hair rising in graceful curves from her full round neck, heightened her beauty to an extraordinary degree.

"As she walked, the clinging folds of her dress, outlining her queenly figure, seemed part of her very being, and to be imbued with her soul. He was dazzled with the new revelation of her power over him."

The fact that she goes for a ride later on, "dressed in pure white," sinks into insignificance beside this new and original creation of Mr. Dixon's. A red morning gown, trimmed with cream lace, cut low enough to show the "beautiful white shoulders"—ye gods and little fishes! Where were the authorities, and why was not "Miss Sallie" taken to the detention hospital, pending an inquiry into her sanity?

It would seem that any man, especially one who writes books, could be sure of a number of women friends. Among these there ought to be at least one whom he could take into his confidence. The gentleman novelist might go to the chosen one and say: "My heroine, in moderate circumstances, is going to the matinée with a girl friend. What shall she wear?"

Instantly the discerning woman would ask the colour of her eyes and hair, and the name of the town she lived in, then behold!

Upon the writer's page would come a radiant feminine vision, clothed in her right mind and in proper clothes, to the joy of every woman who reads the book.

But men are proverbially chary of their confidence, except when they are in love, and being in love is supposed to put even book women out of a man's head. Perhaps in the new Schools of Journalism which are to be inaugurated, there will be supplementary courses in millinery elective, for those who wish to learn the trade of novel writing.

If a man knows no woman to whom he can turn for counsel and advice at the critical point in his book, there are only two courses open to him, aside from the doubtful one of evasion. He may let his fancy run riot and put his heroine into clothes that would give even a dumb woman hysterics, or he may follow the example of Mr. Chatfield-Taylor, who says of one of his heroines that "her pliant body was enshrouded in white muslin with a blue ribbon at the waist."

Lacking the faithful hench-woman who would gladly put them straight, the majority of gentlemen novelists evade the point, and, so far as clothes are concerned, their heroines are as badly off as the Queen of Spain was said to be for legs.

They delve freely into emotional situations, and fearlessly attempt profound psychological problems, but slide off like frightened crabs when they strike the clothesline.

After all, it may be just as well, since fashion is transient and colours and material do not vary much. Still, judging by the painful mistakes that many of them have made, the best advice that one can give the gallant company of literary craftsmen is this: "When you come to millinery, crawfish!"

Maidens of the Sea

Far out in the ocean, deep and blue,
Where the winds dance wild and free,
In coral caves, dwells a beautiful band—
The maidens of the sea.

There are stories old, of the mystic tide,
And legends strange, of the deep,
How the witching sound of the siren's song
Can lull the tempest to sleep.

When moonlight falls on a crystal sea,
When the clouds have backward rolled,
The mermaids sing their low sweet songs,
And their harp strings are of gold.

The billows come from the vast unknown—
From their far-away unseen home;
The waves bring shells to the sandy bar,
And the fairies dance on the foam.

The Technique of the Short Story

An old rule for those who would be well-dressed says: "When you have finished, go to the mirror and see what you can take off." The same rule applies with equal force to the short story: "When you have written it out, go over it carefully, and see what you can take out."

Besides being the best preparation for the writing of novels, short-story writing is undoubtedly, at the present time, the best paying and most satisfactory form of any ephemeral literary work. The qualities which make it successful are to be attained only by constant and patient practice. The real work of writing a story may be brief, but years of preparation must be worked through before a manuscript, which may be written in an hour or so, can present an artistic result.

The first and most important thing to consider is the central idea. There are only a few ideas in the world, but their ramifications are countless, and one need never despair of a theme. Your story may be one of either failure or success, but it must have the true ring. Given the man and the circumstances, we should know his action.

The plot must unfold naturally; otherwise it will be a succession of distinct sensations, rather than a complete and harmonious whole.

There is no better way to produce this effect than to follow Edmund Russell's rule of colour in dress: "When a contrasting colour is introduced, there should be at least two subordinate repetitions of it."

Each character should appear, or be spoken of, at least twice before his main action. Following this rule makes one of the differences between artistic and sensational literature.

The heroine of a dime novel always finds a hero to rescue her in the nick of time, and perhaps she never sees him again. In the artistic novel, while the heroine may see the rescuer first at the time she needs him most, he never disappears altogether from the story.

Description is a thing which is much abused. There is no truer indication of an inexperienced hand than a story beginning with a description of a landscape which is not necessary to the plot. If the peculiarities of the scenery must be understood before the idea can be developed, the briefest possible description is not out of place. Subjectively, a touch of landscape or weather is allowable, but it must be purely incidental. Weather is a very common thing and is apt to be uninteresting.

It is a mistake to tell anything yourself which the people in the story could inform the reader without your assistance. A conversation between two people will bring out all the facts necessary as well as two pages of narration by the author.

There is a way also of telling things from the point of view of the persons which they concern. Those who have studied Latin will find the "indirect discourse" of Cicero a useful model.

The people in the story can tell their own peculiarities better than the author can do it for them. It is not necessary to say that a woman is a snarling, grumpy person. Bring the old lady in, and let her snarl, if she is in your story at all.

The choice of words is not lightly to be considered. Never use two adjectives where one will do, or a weak word where a stronger one is possible. Fallows' *100,000 Synonyms and Antonyms* and Roget's *Thesaurus of Words and Phrases* will prove invaluable to those who wish to improve themselves in this respect.

Analysis of sentences which seem to you particularly strong is a good way to strengthen your vocabulary. Take, for instance, the oft-quoted expression of George Eliot's: "Inclination snatches argument to make indulgence seem judicious choice." Substitute "takes" for "snatches" and read the sentence again. Leave out "seem" and put "appear" in its place. "Proper" is a synonym for "judicious"; substitute it, and put "selection" in the place of "choice."

Reading the sentence again we have: "Inclination takes argument to make indulgence appear proper selection." The strength is wholly gone although the meaning is unchanged.

Find out what you want to say, and then say it, in the most direct English at your command. One of the best models of concise expressions of thought is to be found in the essays of Emerson. He compresses a whole world into a single sentence, and a system of philosophy into an epigram.

"Literary impressionism," which is largely the use of onomatopoetic words, is a valuable factor in the artistic short story. It is possible to convey the impression of a threatening sky and a stormy sea without doing more than alluding to the crash of the surf against the shore. The mind of the reader accustomed to subtle touches will at once picture the rest.

An element of strength is added also by occasionally referring an impression to another sense. For instance, the newspaper poet writes: "The street was white with snow," and makes his line commonplace doggerel. Tennyson says: "The streets were *dumb* with snow," and his line is poetry.

"Blackening the background" is a common fault with story writers. In many of the Italian operas, everybody who does not appear in the final scene is killed off in the middle of the last act. This wholesale slaughter is useless as well as inartistic. The true artist does not, in order that his central figure may stand out prominently, make his background a solid wall of gloom. Yet gloom has its proper place, as well as joy.

In the old tragedies of the Greeks, just before the final catastrophe, the chorus is supposed to advance to the centre of the theatre and sing a bacchanal of frensied exultation.

In the *Antigone* of Sophocles, just before the death of Antigone and her lover, the chorus sings an ode which makes one wonder at its extravagant expression. When the catastrophe occurs, the mystery is explained. Sophocles meant the sacrifice of Antigone to come home with its full force; and well he attained his end by use of an artistic method which few of our writers are subtle enough to recognise and claim for their own purposes.

"High-sounding sentences," which an inexperienced writer is apt to put into the mouths of his people, only make them appear ridiculous. The schoolgirl in the story is too apt to say: "The day has been most unpleasant," whereas the real schoolgirl throws her books down with a bang, and declares that she has "had a perfectly horrid time!"

Her grammar may be incorrect, but her method of expression is true to life, and there the business of the writer ends.

Put yourself in your hero's place and see what you would do under similar circumstances. If you were in love with a young woman, you wouldn't get down on your knees, and swear by all that was holy that you would die if she didn't marry you, at the same time tearing your hair out by handfuls, and then endeavour to give her a concise biography of yourself.

You would put your arm around her, the first minute you had her to yourself, if you felt reasonably sure that she cared for you, and tell her what she meant to you—perhaps so low that even the author of the story couldn't hear what you said, and would have to describe what he saw afterward in order to let his reader guess what had really happened.

It is a lamentable fact that the description of a person's features gives absolutely no idea of his appearance. It is better to give a touch or two, and let the imagination do the rest. "Hair like raven's wing," and the "midnight eyes," and many similar things, may be very well spared. The personal charms of the lover may be brought out through the mediations of the lovee, much better than by pages of description.

The law of compensation must always have its place in the artistic story. Those who do wrong must suffer wrong—those who work must be rewarded, if not in the tangible things they seek, at least in the conscious strength that comes from struggling. And "poetic justice," which metes out to those who do the things that they have done, is relentless and eternal, in art, as well as in life.

"Style" is purely an individual matter, and, if it is anything at all, it is the expression of one's self. Zola has said that, "art is nature seen through the medium of a temperament," and the same is true of literature. Bunner's stories are as thoroughly Bunner as the man who wrote them, and *The Badge of Courage* is nothing unless it be the moody, sensitive, half-morbid Stephen Crane.

Observation of things nearest at hand and the sympathetic understanding of people are the first requisites. Do not place the scene of a story in Europe if you have never been there, and do not assume to comprehend the inner life of a Congressman if you have never seen one. Do not write of mining camps if you have never seen a mountain, or of society if you have never worn evening dress.

James Whitcomb Riley has made himself loved and honoured by writing of the simple things of home, and Louisa Alcott's name is a household word because she wrote of the little women whom she knew. Eugene Field has written of the children that he loved and understood, and won a truer fame than if he had undertaken *The Master* of Zangwill. Kipling's life in India has given us *Plain Tales from the Hills* and *The Jungle Book*, which Mary E. Wilkins could not have written in spite of the genius which made her New England stories the most effective of their kind. Joel Chandler Harris could not have written *The Prisoner of Zenda*, but those of us who have enjoyed the wiles of that "monstus soon beast, Brer Rabbit," would not have it otherwise.

You cannot write of love unless you have loved, of suffering unless you have suffered, or of death unless some one who was near to you has learned the heavenly secret. A little touch of each must teach you the full meaning of the great thing you mean to write about, or your work will be lacking. There are few of us to whom the great experiences do not come sooner or later, and, in the meantime, there are the little everyday happenings, which are full of sweetness and help, if they are only seen properly, to last until the great things come to test our utmost strength, to crush us if we are not strong, and to make us broader, better men and women if we withstand the blow.

And lastly, remember this, that merit is invariably recognised. If your stories are worth printing, they will fight their way through "the abundance of material on hand." The light of the public square is the unfailing test, and a good story is sure to be published sooner or later, if a fair amount of literary instinct is exercised in sending it out. Meteoric success is not desirable. Slow, hard, conscientious work will surely win its way, and those who are now near the bottom of the ladder are gradually ascending to make room for the next generation of story-writers on the rounds below.

To Dorothy

There's a sleepy look in your violet eyes,
So the sails of our ship we'll unfurl,
And turn the prow to the Land of Rest,
My dear little Dorothy girl.

Twilight is coming soon, little one,
The sheep have gone to the fold;
See! where our white sails bend and dip
In the sunset glow of gold.

The roses nod to the sound of the waves,
And the bluebells sweet are ringing;
Do you hear the music, Dorothy dear?
The song that the angels are singing?

The fairies shall weave their drowsy spell
On the shadowy shore of the stream;
Dear little voyager say "good-night,"
For the birds are beginning to dream.

O white little craft, with sails full spread,
My heart goes out with thee;
God keep thee strong with thy precious freight,
My Dorothy—out at sea.

Writing a Book

Having written a few small books which have been published by a reputable house, and which have been pleasantly received by both the press and the public, and having just completed another which I devoutly pray may meet the same fate, I feel that I may henceforth deem myself an author.

I have been considered such for some time among my numerous acquaintances ever since I made my literary bow with a short story in a literary magazine, years and years ago. Being of the feminine persuasion, I am usually presented to strangers as "an authoress." It is at these times that I wish I were a man.

The social side of authorship is extremely interesting. At least once a week, I am asked how I "came to write."

This is difficult, for I do not know. When I so reply, my questioner ascertains by further inquiries where I was educated and how I have been trained. Never having been through a "School of Journalism," my answer is not satisfactory.

"You must read a great deal in order to get all those ideas," is frequently said to me. I reply that I do read a great deal, being naturally bookish, but that it is the great object of my life to avoid getting ideas from books. To an author, "Plagiarist" is like the old cry of "Wolf," and when an idea is once assimilated it is difficult indeed to distinguish it from one's own.

I am often asked how long it takes me to write a book. I am ashamed to tell, but sometimes the secret escapes, since I am naturally truthful, and find it hard to parry a direct question. The actual time of composition is always greeted with astonishment, and I can read the questioner's inference, that if I can do so much in so short a time, how much could I do if I actually worked!

This is always distasteful, so I hasten to add that the composition is really a very small part of the real writing of a book, and that authors' methods differ. My own practice is not to begin to write until my material is fully arranged in my mind, and I often use notes which I have been making for a period of months. Such a report is seldom convincing, however, to my questioners. I am gradually learning, when this inquiry comes, to smile inscrutably.

It seems strange to many people that I do not work all the time. If I can write a short story in two hours and be paid thirty dollars for it, I am an idiot indeed if I do not write at least three in a day! Ninety dollars a day might easily mount up into a very comfortable income.

Still, there are some who understand that an author cannot write continuously any more than a spider or a silkworm can spin all the time. These people ask me when, and where, and how, I get my material.

"Getting material" is supposed to be a secret process, and I am thought a gay deceiver when I say I make no particular effort to get it—that it comes in the daily living—like the morning cream! I am then asked if I rely wholly upon "inspiration." I answer that "inspiration" doubtless has its value as well as hard work, and that the author who would derive all possible benefit from the rare flashes of it must have the same command of technique that a good workman has of his tools.

The majority learn with surprise that there is more to a book than is self-evident. It was once my happy lot to put this fact into the understanding of a lady from the country.

With infinite pains I told her of the constant study of words, illustrated the fine shades of distinction between synonyms, spoke of the different ways in which characters and events might be introduced, and of the subordinate repetition of contrasting themes. She listened in breathless wonder, and then turned to her daughter: "There, Mame," she said, "I told you there was something in it!"

There is nothing so pathetic as the widespread literary ambition among people whose future is utterly hopeless. It is sad enough for one who has attained a small success to see the heights which are ever beyond, and it makes one gentle indeed to those who come seeking aid.

One ambitious soul once asked me if I would teach her to write. I replied that I did not know of any way in which it could be taught, but that I would gladly help her if I could. She said she had absolutely no imagination, and asked me if that would make any difference. I told her it was certainly an unfortunate circumstance and advised her to cultivate that quality before she attempted extensive writing. I suppose she is still doing it, for I have not been asked for further assistance.

People often inquire what qualities I deem essential to literary success. Imagination is, of course, the first, observation, the second, and ambition, perseverance and executive ability are indispensable. Besides these I would place the sense of humour, of proportion, sympathy, insight,—indeed, there is nothing admirable in human nature which would come amiss in the equipment of a writer.

The necessity for the humourous sense was recently brought home to me most forcibly. A woman brought me the manuscript of a novel which she asked me to read. She felt that something was wrong with it, but she did not know just what it was. She said it needed "a few little touches," she thought, such as my experience would have fitted me to give, and she would be grateful, indeed, if I would revise it. She added that, owing to the connection which I had formed with my publishing house, it would be an easy matter for me to get it published, and she generously offered to divide the royalties with me if I would consummate the arrangement!

I began to read the manuscript, and had not gone far when I discovered that it was indeed rare. The entire family read it, or portions of it, with screams of laughter, and with tears in their eyes, although it was not intended to be a funny book at all. To this day, certain phrases from that novel will upset any one of us, even at a solemn time.

Of course it was badly written. Characters appeared, talked for a few pages, and were never seen or heard from again.

Long conversations were intruded which had no connection with such plot as there was. Commonplace descriptions of scenery, also useless, were frequent. Many a time the thread of the story was lost. There were no distinguishing traits in any one of the characters—they all talked very much alike. But the supreme defect was the author's lack of humour. With all seriousness, she made her people say and do things which were absolutely ridiculous and not by any means true to life.

I think I must have an unsuspected bit of tact somewhere for I extricated myself from the situation, and the woman is still my friend. I did not hurt her feelings about her book, nor did I send it to my publishers with a letter of recommendation. I remarked that her central idea was all right, which was true, since it was a love story, but that it had not been properly developed and that she needed to study. She thanked me for my counsel and said she would rewrite it. I wish it might be printed just as it was, however, for it is indeed a sodden and mirthless world in which we live and move.

As the editors say on the refusal blanks, "I am always glad to read manuscripts," although, as a rule, it makes an enemy for me if I try to help the author by criticism, when only praise was expected or desired.

Having written some verse which has landed in respectable places, I am also asked about poetry. Poems written in trochaic metre with the good old rhymes, "trees and breeze," "light and night," soldered on at the end of the lines, are continually brought to me for revision and improvement.

Once, for the benefit of the literary aspirant, I brought out my rhyming dictionary, but I shall never do it again. He looked it over carefully, while I explained the advantage for the writer in having before him all the available rhymes, so that the least common might be quickly chosen and the verse made to run smoothly.

"Humph!" he said; "it's just the book. Anybody can write poetry with one of these books!"

My invaluable thesaurus is chained to my desk in order that it may not escape, and I frequently have to justify its existence when aliens penetrate my den. "It's no wonder you can write," was said to me once. "Here's all the English language right on your desk, and all you've got to do is to put it together."

"Yes," I answered wickedly, "but it's all in the dictionary too."

Last week I had a rare treat. I met a woman who had "never seen a literary person before," and who said "it was quite a novelty!" I beamed upon her, for it is very nice to be a "novelty," and after a while we became quite confidential.

"I want you to tell me just how you write," she said, "so's I can tell the folks at home. I'm going to buy some of your books to give away."

Mindful of "royalty to author," I immediately became willing to tell anything I could.

"Well, I want to know how you write. Do you just sit down and do it?"

"Yes, I just sit down and do it."

"Do you write any special time?"

"No, mornings, usually; but any time will do."

"What do you write with—a pen or a pencil?"

"Neither, I always use a typewriter."

"Why, can you write on a typewriter?"

"Yes, it's much easier than a pen, and it keeps the ink off your hands. You can write with both hands at once, you know."

"You have to write it all out with a pencil, first, don't you?"

"No, I just think into the keys."

"Wouldn't it be easier to write it with a pencil first and then copy it?"

"No, or I'd do it that way."

"Do you dress any special way when you write?"

"No, only I must be neat and also comfortable. I usually wear a shirt-waist and take off my collar. Can't write with a collar on, but I must be well groomed otherwise."

There was a long silence. The little lady was digesting the information which she had just received.

"It seems easy enough," she said. "I should think any one could write. What do you do when it is done?"

"Oh, I go all over it and revise very carefully."

"Why, do you have to go all over it, after it is done?"

"Certainly."

"Then it takes you longer than it does most people, doesn't it?"

"I cannot say as to that. Everybody revises."

"Why, when I write a letter, if I go over it I always scratch out so much that I have to do it over."

"That's the idea, exactly," I replied. "I go over it until there isn't a thing to be scratched out, or a word to be changed."

"But you've got lots left," she said, enviously. "When I go over a letter there's hardly anything left."

Innumerable questions followed these, but at last she had her curiosity partially satisfied and turned away from me. I trust, however, that I shall some day meet her again, for she too is "a novelty!"

The mechanical part of a book is a source of great wonder to the uninitiated. My galley proofs were once passed around among the guests at a summer hotel as if they were some new strange animal. They did not understand page proofs nor plates, nor how I could ever know when it was right.

The cover is frequently commented upon as a thing of beauty (which with my publishers it always is), and I am asked if I did it. I am always sorry that I do not know enough to do covers, so I have to explain that an artist does that—that I often do not see it until the first copies come from the bindery, and that I am of such small importance that I am not often consulted in relation to the matter—being merely the poor worm who wrote the book.

There are many people who seem to be afraid to talk before me lest their pearly utterances be transformed into copy. Time and time again I have heard this: "We must be very careful what we say now, or Miss —— will put us into a book!"

People are strangely literal. An author gets no credit whatever for inventive faculty—his characters and stories are supposedly real people and real things. I am asked how I came to know so much about such and such a thing. I once wrote a love story with an unhappy ending and it was at once assumed that I had been disappointed in love!

When my first book came from the press I was pointed out at a reception as the author of it. The man surveyed me long and carefully, then he announced: "That's a mistake. That girl never wrote that book. She's too frivolous and empty headed!"

I have tried, until I am discouraged, to make people understand that a book does not have to be a verity in order to be true—that a story must be possible, instead of actual, and that actual circumstances may be too unreal for literature.

There are always people who will ask that things, even books, may be written especially for them. People often want to tell me a story and let me write it up into a nice book and divide the royalties with them! During a summer at the coast, I had endless opportunities to write biographical sketches of the guests at the hotel—to write a story and put them all into it, or to write something about anything, that they might have as "a souvenir!" As a matter of fact, there were only two people at the hotel who could have been of any possible use as copy, and one of these was a woman to whom only Mr. Stockton could have done justice.

It was hard to be always good-natured, but I lost my temper only once. We stayed late into the autumn and were rewarded by a magnificent storm. I put on my bathing suit and my mackintosh and went down to the beach, in the teeth of a northwest gale. Little needles of sand were blown in my face, and I lost my cap, but it was well worth the effort. For over an hour we stood on the desolate beach, sheltered from the sand by a bath house. I had never seen anything so grand—it was far beyond words. At last it grew dark and I was soaked through and stiff with the cold. So I went back to the hotel, my soul struck dumb by the might and glory of the sea. My heart was too full to speak. The majestic chords were still thundering in my ears; that tempest-tossed ocean was still before my eyes. On my way upstairs I met a woman whom I had formerly liked.

"Oh, Miss ——, I want you to write me a description of that storm!" I brushed past her, rudely, I fear, and she caught hold of the cape of my mackintosh with elephantine playfulness. "You can't go," she said coquettishly, "until you promise to write me a description of that storm!"

"I can't write it," I said coldly. "Please let me go."

"You've got to write it," she returned. "I know you can, and I won't let you go until you promise me."

I wrenched myself away from her, white with wrath, and got to my room before she did, though she was still pursuing me. I locked my door and had a hard fight for my self-control. From the beach came the distant boom of the surf, mingled with the liquid melody of the returning breakers.

Later, just as I had finished dressing for dinner, there was a tap at my door. My friend (?) stood there beaming. "Have you got it done? You know you promised to write me a description of that storm!"

She remained only three days longer, and I stayed away from her as much as possible, but occasional meetings were inevitable. When the gladsome time of parting came, she hung about my neck.

"I want you to come and see me," she said. "You know you haven't done what you said you would. Don't you forget to write me a description of that storm!"

My business arrangements with my publishers are seemingly a matter of public interest. I am asked how much it costs to print a book the size of mine. People are surprised to find that I do not pay the expenses and that I haven't the least idea of what it costs.

Then they want to know if the publisher buys the book of me. I explain that this is sometimes done, but that I myself am paid upon the royalty basis, — — per cent. on the list price of every copy sold. This seems painfully small to the dear public, but it is comparatively easy to demonstrate that the royalty on five or six thousand copies is quite worth while.

They shortly come to the conclusion, however, that the publishers make more money than I do, and that seems to them to be very unfair. They suggest that if I published it myself, I should make a great deal more money!

It is difficult for them to understand that writing books and selling books are two very different propositions—that I don't know enough to sell books, and that the imprint of a reputable house upon the title-page is worth a great deal to any author.

"Well," a man once said to me, "how much did you make out of your book this year?"

I explained that the percentage royalty basis was really an equal division of the profits, everything considered, and that all the financial risk was on one side. I named my few hundreds, with which I was very well satisfied. He absorbed himself in a calculation on the back of an envelope.

"I figure out," said he, at length, "that they must have made at least a third more than you did. That isn't fair!"

My ire arose. "It is perfectly fair," I replied. "Paper is cheap, I know, but composition isn't, and advertising isn't. They are welcome to every penny they can make out of my books. I'd be glad to have them make twice as much as they do now, even if my own income remained the same."

At this point, I became telepathically aware that I was considered crazy, so I changed the subject.

I am often asked how I happened to meet my publishers and "get in with them," and as a very great favour to me, and to them, I am offered the privilege of sending them some "splendid novel which was written by a friend" of somebody—as they know me, "they have decided to let my publishers have the book!"

They are surprised to hear me say that I have never met any member of the firm, though I was in the same city with them for over a year. More than this, there is nothing on earth, except a green worm, which would scare me so much as a summons to that publishing house.

I have walked by in fear and trembling. I have seen a huge pile of my books in the window, and on the bulletin board a poster which bore my name in conspicuous letters, as if I had been cured of something. But I should no more dare to go into that office than I should venture to call upon the wife of the President with a shawl over my head, and my fancywork tucked under my arm.

This is incomprehensible to the uninitiated. The publishers have ever been most courteous and kind. They are people with whom it is a pleasure to have any sort of business dealings, but we are not bosom friends—and I very much fear that they do not care to become chummy with me.

There may be some authors who have taken nerve tonics and are not afraid to meet an editor or publisher. I have even read of some who will walk cheerfully into an editorial sanctum—but I've never seen a sanctum, nor an editor, nor a publisher. I don't even write to an editor when I send him a piece—just put in a stamp. He usually knows what to do with it.

Fame, or long experience, may enable authors to meet the arbiters of their destiny without becoming frightened, but I have had brief experience, and still less fame. The admirable qualities of the pachyderm may have been bestowed upon some authors—but not on this one.

The Man Behind the Gun

Now let the eagle flap his wings
And let the cannon roar,
For while the conquering bullet sings
We pledge the commodore.
First battle of a righteous war
Right royally he won,
But here's a health to the jolly tar—
To the man behind the gun!

Now praise be to the flag-ship's spars—
To the captain in command,
And honour to the Stripes and Stars
For whose defence they stand;
And for the pilot at his wheel
Let the streams of red wine run,
But here's a health to the man of steel—
The man behind the gun!

Here's to the man who does not swerve
In the face of any foe;
Here's to the man of iron nerve,
On deck and down below;
Here's to the man whose heart is glad
When the battle has begun;
Here's to the health of that daring lad—
To the man behind the gun!

Now let the Stars and Stripes float high
And let the eagle soar;
Until the echoes make reply
We pledge the commodore.
Here's to the chief and here's to war,
And here's to the fleet that won,
And here's a health to the jolly tar—
To the man behind the gun!

Quaint Old Christmas Customs

Compared with the celebrations of our ancestors, the modern Christmas becomes a very hurried thing. The rush of the twentieth century forbids twelve days of celebration, or even two. Paterfamilias considers himself very indulgent if he gives two nights and a day to the annual festival, because, forsooth, "the office needs him!"

One by one the quaint old customs have vanished. We still have the Christmas tree, evergreens in our houses and churches, and the yawning stocking still waits in many homes for the good St. Nicholas.

But what is poor Santa Claus to do when the chimney leads to the furnace? And what of the city apartment, which boasts a radiator and gas grate, but no chimney? The myth evidently needs reconstruction to meet the times in which we live, and perhaps we shall soon see pictures of Santa Claus arriving in an automobile, and taking the elevator to the ninth floor, flat B, where a single childish stocking is hung upon the radiator.

Nearly all of the Christmas observances began in ancient Rome. The primitive Italians were wont to celebrate the winter solstice and call it the feast of Saturn. Thus Saturnalia came to mean almost any kind of celebration which came in the wake of conquest, and these ceremonies being engrafted upon Anglo-Saxon customs assumed a religious significance.

The pretty maid who hesitates and blushes beneath the overhanging branch of mistletoe, never stops to think of the grim festival with which the Druids celebrated its gathering.

In their mythology the plant was regarded with the utmost reverence, especially when found growing upon an oak.

At the time of the winter solstice, the ancient Britons, accompanied by their priests, the Druids, went out with great pomp and rejoicing to gather the mistletoe, which was believed to possess great curative powers. These processions were usually by night, to the accompaniment of flaring torches and the solemn chanting of the people. When an oak was reached on which the parasite grew, the company paused.

Two white bulls were bound to the tree and the chief Druid, clothed in white to signify purity, climbed, more or less gracefully, to the plant. It was severed from the oak, and another priest, standing below, caught it in the folds of his robe. The bulls were then sacrificed, and often, alas, human victims also. The mistletoe thus gathered was divided into small portions and distributed among the people. The tiny sprays were fastened above the doors of the houses, as propitiation to the sylvan deities during the cold season.

These rites were retained throughout the Roman occupation of Great Britain, and for some time afterward, under the sovereignty of the Jutes, the Saxons, and the Angles.

In Scandinavian mythology there is a beautiful legend of the mistletoe. Balder, the god of poetry, the son of Odin and Friga, one day told his mother that he had dreamed his death was near at hand. Much alarmed, the mother invoked all the powers of nature—earth, air, water, fire, animals and plants, and obtained from them a solemn oath that they would do her son no harm.

Then Balder fearlessly took his place in the combats of the gods and fought unharmed while showers of arrows were falling all about him.

His enemy, Loake, determined to discover the secret of his invulnerability, and, disguising himself as an old woman, went to the mother with a question of the reason of his immunity. Friga answered that she had made a charm and invoked all nature to keep from injuring her son.

"Indeed," said the old woman, "and did you ask all the animals and plants? There are so many, it seems impossible."

"All but one," answered Friga proudly; "all but a little insignificant plant which grows upon the bark of the oak. This I did not think of invoking, since so small a thing could do no harm."

Much delighted, Loake went away and gathered mistletoe. Then he entered the assembly of the gods and made his way to the blind Heda.

"Why do you not shoot with the arrows at Balder?" asked Loake.

"Alas," replied Heda, "I am blind and have no arms."

Loake then gave him an arrow tipped with mistletoe and said: "Balder is before thee." Heda shot and Balder fell, pierced through the heart.

In its natural state, the plant is believed to be propagated by the missel-thrush, which feeds upon its berries, but under favourable climatic conditions one may raise one's own mistletoe by bruising the berries on the bark of fruit trees, where they take root readily. It must be remembered, however, that the plant is a true parasite and will eventually kill whatever tree gives it nourishment.

Kissing under the mistletoe was also a custom of the Druids, and in those uncivilised days men kissed each other. For each kiss, a single white berry was plucked from the spray, and kept as a souvenir by the one who was kissed.

The burning of the Yule log was an ancient Christmas ceremony borrowed from the early Scandinavians. At their feast of Juul (pronounced *Yuul*), at the time of the winter solstice, they were wont to kindle huge bonfires in honour of their god Thor. The custom soon made its way to England where it is still in vogue in many parts of the country.

One may imagine an ancient feudal castle, heavily fortified, standing in splendid isolation upon a snowy hill, on that night of all others when war was forgotten and peace proclaimed. Drawn by six horses, the great Yule log was brought into the hall and rolled into the vast fireplace, where it was lighted with the charred remnants of last year's Yule log, religiously kept in some secure place as a charm against fire.

As the flames seize upon the oak and the light gleams from the castle windows, a lusty procession of wayfarers passes through, each one raising his hat as he passes the fire which burns all the evil out of the hearts of men, and up to the rafters there rings a stern old Saxon chant.

When the song was finished, the steaming wassail bowl was brought out, and all the company drank to a better understanding.

Up to the time of Henry VI, and even afterward, the Yule log was greeted with bards and minstrelsy. If a squinting person came into the hall while the log was burning, it was sure to bring bad luck. The appearance of a barefooted man was worse, and a flat-footed woman was the worst of all.

As an accompaniment to the Yule log, a monstrous Christmas candle was burned on the table at supper; even now in St. John's College at Oxford, there is an old candle socket of stone, ornamented with the figure of a lamb. What generations of gay students must have sat around that kindly light when Christmas came to Oxford!

Snap-dragon was a favourite Christmas sport at this time. Several raisins were put into a large shallow bowl and thoroughly saturated with brandy. All other lights were extinguished and the brandy ignited. By turns each one of the company tried to snatch a raisin out of the flames, singing meanwhile.

In Devonshire, they burn great bundles of ash sticks, while master and servants sit together, for once on terms of perfect equality, and drink spiced ale, and the season is one of great rejoicing.

Another custom in Devonshire is for the farmer, his family, and friends, to partake of hot cake and cider, and afterward go to the orchard and place a cake ceremoniously in the fork of a big tree, when cider is poured over it while the men fire off pistols and the women sing.

A similar libation, but of spiced ale, used to be sprinkled through the orchards and meadows of Norfolk. Midnight of Christmas was the time usually chosen for the ceremony.

In Devon and Cornwall, a belief is current that, at midnight on Christmas Eve, the cattle kneel in their stalls in honour of the Saviour, as legend claims they did in Bethlehem.

In Wales, they carry about at Christmas time a horse's skull gaily adorned with ribbons, and supported on a pole by a man who is wholly concealed by a white cloth. There is a clever contrivance for opening and shutting the jaws, and this strange creature pursues and bites all who come near it.

The figure is usually accompanied by a party of men and boys grotesquely dressed, who, on reaching a house, sing some verses, often extemporaneous, demanding admittance, and are answered in the same fashion by those within until rhymes have given out on one side or the other.

In Scotland, he who first opens the door on Christmas Day expects more good luck than will fall to the lot of other members of the family during the year, because, as the saying goes, he lets in Yule.

In Germany, Christmas Eve is the children's night, and there is a tree and presents. England and America appear to have borrowed the Christmas tree from Germany, where the custom is ancient and very generally followed.

In the smaller towns and villages in northern Germany, the presents are sent by all the parents to some one fellow who, in high buskins, white robe, mask, and flaxen wig, personates the servant, Rupert. On Christmas night he goes around to every house, and says that his master sent him. The parents and older children receive him with pomp and reverence, while the younger ones are often badly frightened.

He asks for the children, and then demands of their parents a report of their conduct during the past year. The good children are rewarded with sugar-plums and other things, while for the bad ones a rod is given to the parents with instructions to use it freely during the coming year.

In those parts of Pennsylvania where there are many German settlers, the little sinners often find birchen rods suggestively placed in their stockings on Christmas morning.

In Poland, the Christmas gifts are hidden, and the members of the family search for them.

In Sweden and Norway, the house is thoroughly cleaned, and juniper or fir branches are spread over the floor. Then each member of the family goes in turn to the bake house, or outer shed, where he takes his annual bath.

But it is back to Old England, after all, that we look for the merriest Christmas. For two or three weeks beforehand, men and boys of the poorer class, who were called "waits," sang Christmas carols under every window.

Until quite recently these carols were sung all through England, and others of similar import were heard in France and Italy.

The English are said to "take their pleasures sadly," but in the matter of Christmas they can "give us cards and spades and still win." Parties of Christmas drummers used to go around to the different houses, grotesquely attired, and play all sorts of tricks. The actors were chiefly boys, and the parish beadle always went along to insure order.

The Christmas dinner of Old England was a thing capable of giving the whole nation dyspepsia if they indulged freely.

The main dish was a boar's head, roasted to a turn, and preceded by trumpets and minstrelsy. Mustard was indispensable to this dish.

Next came a peacock, skinned and roasted. The beak was gilded, and sometimes a bit of cotton, well soaked in spirits, was put into his mouth, and when he was brought to the table this was ignited, so that the bird was literally spouting fire. He was stuffed with spices, basted with yolks of eggs, and served with plenty of gravy.

Geese, capons, pheasants, carps' tongues, frumenty, and mince, or "shred" pies, made up the balance of the feast.

The chief functionary of Christmas was called "The Lord of Misrule."

In the house of king and nobleman he held full sway for twelve days. His badge was a fool's bauble and he was always attended by a page, both of them being masked. So many pranks were played, and so much mischief perpetrated which was far from being amusing, that an edict was eventually issued against this form of liberty, not to say license.

The Lord of Misrule was especially reviled by the Puritans, one of whom set him down as "a grande captain of mischiefe." One may easily imagine that this stern old gentleman had been ducked by a party of revellers following in the wake of the lawless "Captaine" because he had refused to contribute to their entertainment.

We need not lament the passing of Christmas pageantry, if the spirit of the festival remains. Through the centuries that have passed since the first Christmas, the spirit of it has wandered in and out like a golden thread in a dull tapestry, sometimes hidden, but never wholly lost. It behooves us to keep well and reverently such Christmas as we have, else we shall share old Ben Jonson's lament in *The Mask of Father Christmas*, which was presented before the English Court nearly two hundred years ago:

"Any man or woman ... that can give any knowledge, or tell any tidings of an old, very old, grey haired gentleman called Christmas, who was wont to be a very familiar ghest, and visit all sorts of people both pore and rich, and used to appear in glittering gold, silk and silver in the court, and in all shapes in the theatre in Whitehall, and had singing, feasts and jolitie in all places, both citie and countrie for his coming—whosoever can tel what is become of him, or where he may be found, let them bring him back again into England."

Consecration

Cathedral spire and lofty architrave,
Nor priestly rite and humble reverence,
Nor costly fires of myrrh and frankincense
May give the consecration that we crave;
Upon the shore where tides forever lave
With grateful coolness on the fevered sense;
Where passion grows to silence, rapt, intense,
There waits the chrismal fountain of the wave.

By rock-hewn altars where is said no word,
Save by the deep that calleth unto deep,
While organ tones of sea resound above;
The truth of truths our inmost souls have heard,
And in our hearts communion wine we keep,
For He Himself hath said it—"God is Love!"

Milton Keynes UK
Ingram Content Group UK Ltd.
UKHW042301170324
439575UK00004B/402